THE LADY *at* BATOCHE

THE LADY *at* BATOCHE

DAVID RICHARDS

THISTLEDOWN PRESS

Canadian Cataloguing in Publication Data
Richards, David, 1953–
The lady at Batoche
ISBN 1-895449-87-1
I. Title.
PS8585.I173 L34 1999 C813'.54 C99-920054-2
PR9199.3.R4649 L34 1999

Cover painting: *Dumont's Scouts* by Armand Paquette
reproduced with permission, Parks Canada,
Batoche National Historic Site.

Typeset by Thistledown Press
Printed and bound in Canada

Thistledown Press Ltd.
633 Main Street
Saskatoon, Saskatchewan
S7H 0J8

Saskatchewan
Arts Board

THE CANADA COUNCIL | LE CONSEIL DES ARTS
FOR THE ARTS | DU CANADA
SINCE 1957 | DEPUIS 1957

Canadian   Patrimoine
Heritage   canadien

Thistledown Press gratefully acknowledges the financial assistance of the Canada Council for the Arts, the Saskatchewan Arts Board, and the Government of Canada through the Book Publishing Industry Development Program for its publishing program.

To Stella, Louise, and James

I would like to thank Phyllis Eagle-Boadway and the Cree community for their editorial advice on First Nations language.

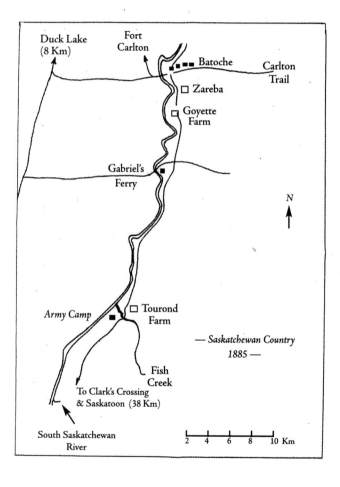

Duck Lake
(8 Km)

Fort
Carlton

Batoche

Carlton
Trail

☐ Zareba

☐ Goyette
Farm

Gabriel's
Ferry

N

Army Camp

☐ Tourond
Farm

— *Saskatchewan Country*
1885 —

Fish
Creek

To Clark's Crossing
& Saskatoon (38 Km)

South Saskatchewan
River

2   4   6   8   10 Km

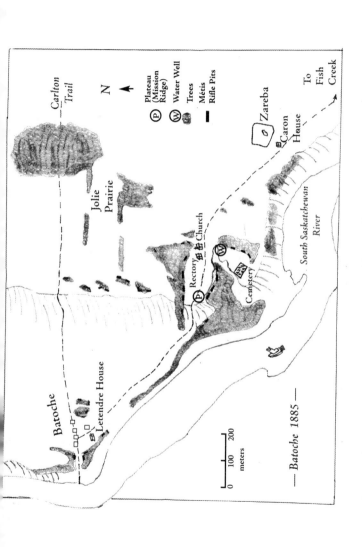

Carlton Trail

Jolie Prairie

N

Plateau (Mission Ridge)
Ⓟ Water Well
Ⓦ Trees
Métis Rifle Pits

Batoche

Letendre House

Rectory 🏠 🏠 Church
Ⓟ
Ⓦ
Cemetery

Zareba
🏠 Caron House

South Saskatchewan River

To Fish Creek

0 100 200
meters

— Batoche 1885 —

Contents

1
TURMOIL

M ail boys! We got mail!"
A young soldier built like a grizzly bear
roared the news from the edge of the army camp.
He ran down the long rows of white bell-shaped
tents, darting here and there repeating his
message.

"Mail for the Winnipeg Rifles!"

He paused outside the second last tent and
poked his head through the door flap.

"Didn't you hear me? Mail, Alex — it's finally
caught up with us."

A wiry little soldier pushed past the bear and
stepped out, straightening his glengarry cap.

"Walter Grayson," he shot a skeptical glance
at the big man. "If this is one o' your pranks, so
help me . . . "

"I wouldn't joke about this, Alex. Come ON!
Our first mail since we left Winnipeg. How long
is that? Must be, ah . . . "

13

"Over a month," Alex said. "Let's go then."

"Wait," Walter caught his arm. "Where's Tom?"

Alex pointed north across a wide, grassy meadow to a line of trees that marked the edge of a river valley.

"Oh, the river again is it?" Walter's voice lost some of its cheer.

"Aye, ever since drill finished. Seems like he spends all his time there now — he's got himself into a right miserable state has our Thomas."

Walter scratched himself thoughtfully. "He's just a kid, eh? Watching his best friend die with a bullet in the guts — well, it's bound to hit him hard."

"Moping about on his own won't help the young pup," Alex answered confidently. "It's up to the regiment — us — to make him buck up. He's got a lot of pluck: remember how he stowed away on the train from home?"

Walter belly laughed. "Staggered out of that boxcar puffed up with frostbite, clutching his bugle and thinking nobody would notice!"

"That's what I mean," Alex said. "He's got grit. He just has to get hold of himself. Come on, we'll smarten him up."

They set off toward the trees.

"Bugler Kerslake! Show yourself, it's mail parade!" Alex yelled.

"Tommy, let's go boy. There's bound to be a letter for you."

A dark green uniform of the 90th Battalion Winnipeg Rifles emerged from the leafless trees. The soldier was small, a boy; he carried a brass trumpet that showed bright against the nearly black uniform. He waved the horn at them.

A laughing mob of soldiers crowded round an open wagon. The fat quartermaster was crouched in the wagon box fumbling through a canvas mailbag trying to sort the last of the letters. They bombarded him with catcalls and rocked the wagon.

"RIGHT! NOBODY gets mail til I get some order here!"

Colour Sergeant James Kerslake only had to bellow once as he pushed his way into the men. They parted quickly to let him pass. Tall, straight-backed as a lance and immaculate in his snug-fitting uniform, he was the picture of a soldier. He was also the Sergeant Major of G Company and the men obeyed him without question. He leaped into the wagon. The quartermaster gave him a bundle of envelopes, then he jumped down.

"G Company! Follow me."

Thirty men detached themselves from the mob and followed him like eager ducklings as he strode back to the half dozen tents that were G Company's home.

"Come forward as I call your name."

He flipped through the bundle.

"Well, well," he smiled. "First one for Colour Sergeant Kerslake — lucky me."

The men groaned impatiently.

"Suppose I could read it later, eh boys?" He tucked it into his belt.

"Next is for Tom Kerslake, my nephew and our esteemed bugler."

Tom darted forward.

"Alexander Laidlaw." The Sergeant Major held up a rose-coloured envelope. Alex strolled with exaggerated calm and retrieved it, holding it carelessly as though it was of little concern to him. Walter's big paw snatched the letter up and held it to his nose, giving a long sniff.

"OOOOOh EEEE, boys! A heavenly scent if ever I smelled one!"

Laidlaw leaped at him, ready to fight.

"Grayson!" Tom's uncle barked once and the letter went back to its red-faced owner.

"Tom Kerslake again, wait . . . and another one."

Tom took them self-consciously as the men hooted.

"Unfair!" "CSM's favourite!" "Humbug — three for him and none for us!"

Jim began delivery in earnest. Mail for the soldiers was precious. They were camped in the Saskatchewan wilderness far from home and did not know if they would ever see that home again. As each man received his letter he scurried away like a thief with treasure. These treasures were to be savoured, read slowly and every word devoured. The crowd began to melt away as the stack of envelopes diminished.

Tom hung back, waiting for his uncle to finish so they could share their news. The CSM called the names quickly now for it was clear there would be several men without mail and he instinctively tried to lessen their disappointment and embarrassment.

"Smith."

"Still in hospital, Sarn't Major," Corporal Snell, with no letters of his own, replied. "I'll take it to him."

"Morrison — Fennel — Flaherty . . . "

Tom's body twitched as though he'd been slapped.

"Oh Lord," Jim was for once caught in confusion. A regretful horror sneaked into his voice. "Um, yes. I will return that one to battalion headquarters."

Tom knew it would be a letter from Paddy Flaherty's mother. Written while she thought her son was still alive. He felt sick. His own letters seemed suddenly heavy. Avoiding his uncle's eye, Tom turned and walked rapidly out of the camp. Mind numb, his feet took him to his place by the river. Just below the top of the bank he reached a small patch of long dry grass and sank into it. He braced his back against a stack of logs he'd built there as a resting place.

The clearing was bounded on three sides by poplar trees but the fourth side was open and gave a clear view of the valley below. The South Saskatchewan River, muddy in its spring flood, rushed through wide, steep banks. To his right a deep notch cut through the bank where a creek — Fish Creek — emptied into the river.

How had Paddy's mother taken the news of his death? Did she even know yet — had their mail reached Winnipeg? He thought of Winnipeg and his own home. So safe, so secure and warm. Normal and predictable. His father would be getting back from work about now. Violet would have supper ready. His sister was an excellent cook — not that he ever gave her credit for it. My God, if only he could be home now; he would praise her cooking to heaven. Would he get that chance? Paddy's mother would never cook for her son again.

Then the ceaseless questions that drove him here every day started up again. Why Paddy? Why not that brute Snell? Why not Tom Kerslake? Or his Uncle? Why had the rebels chosen to kill Paddy? It couldn't be fair — Paddy was the best of them. What kind of God would let him die and keep the rest alive?

He tore open one of the letters, urging his mind back home — before all this Métis rebellion. It was from Vi.

Winnipeg, Manitoba
April 26, 1885
My dearest Tom,
We just heard the news of the Fish Creek battle.
It was reported in the paper in horrid detail. We
thanked God to learn you are safe. It is diffi-
cult to describe our shock when we read of your
exploits in the battle.
We were told you would be kept out of the
fighting yet the paper was full of Bugler Kerslake
— fourteen years old — saving his Corporal in
hand to hand fighting — charging rebel fortifi-
cations! Tom, how could you? It scared us
nearly to death. Father has telegraphed Ottawa
demanding an explanation. He is asking for
your withdrawal from service with the 90th
Battalion. The army can manage with one less
bugler but we could not survive if you were lost
to us.

Tom stopped reading. Go home? Leave the regiment? Not until he had an answer to his questions. Not until he made sense of Paddy's death.
Voices approached the top of the riverbank
behind him. He slithered down behind the logs.

"Where does he go anyway? Do you know for sure?"

It was his uncle. Jim was the best man he knew and it was Jim who had pulled G Company through the battle. But Tom needed time with his thoughts — alone. He stayed hidden.

"Down here somewhere, Grayson says," Snell answered. "But maybe it's best just to leave him be."

"He's brooding on young Flaherty's death. It's not healthy anymore. I should have talked to him before now." Jim's voice was directly above Tom.

"He's tough, Sarn't Major. I gave him a right nasty time on the march up from Qu'Appelle and he took it." Snell hawked and spat. "Then look at the battle. He fought like a prize rooster — all the boys respect him. My advice is let him alone. He'll get over Flaherty once we leave here and go after the half-breeds again. If you baby him now, maybe he'll spoil."

A silence followed. Tom was suddenly fascinated by the discussion. He'd never seen himself quite like Snell described.

"He's a boy, Corporal." A warning lurked in Jim's reply. "A young boy who's had a hard knock. I agree he doesn't need babying: perhaps we've

21

gone too far that way. A bit of discipline might help but I'm also his father's brother. I've got to look out for him."

"Maybe," Snell shot back quickly. "But I know the cure for young Tom — it's revenge. Let him see a couple of rebels go down with a bellyful of lead and he'll be right as . . . "

"That's enough of that kind of talk, Corporal." The full authority of the Sergeant Major came from Jim. "I'll not have you twisting him up with those notions. Discipline and hard work will do the trick."

"Yes, sir," Snell replied calmly. "Beg pardon, sir."

"We'll start now," Jim said briskly. "Muster a work party. We will finish the stonework on Flaherty's grave. Tom can help — maybe it will let him put Paddy to rest."

They moved along the bank and their voices faded. Tom rose to one knee and stared down-river where the broad Saskatchewan valley curved to the horizon. The army would follow it to the Métis capital, Batoche. He imagined the rebel village burning amid exploding shells — the enemy fleeing in defeat. Perhaps Snell was right about revenge.

※ ※ ※

The tip of the needle pierced the stiff, white cotton and sparkled for an instant before Marie's fingers plucked it up. The trailing thread — orange — stretched taut on the cloth as her thimble plunged the needle back down. Then up and down again; up and down. Each neat stitch was perfectly spaced and gradually traced the outline of a lily petal onto the shirt. The blouse would be decorated with three identical flowers intertwined down the centre. She didn't watch her hands or even think about them. They did their job without her interference. She concentrated on the flow of the thread. Where her eyes went, the needle and her fingers followed.

"The council of the Provisional Government suspects the priests are spies — traitors!"

A man's voice lifted up through the stairwell into the loft. Marie tried to shut it out. She filled her mind with the image of a prairie lily and mentally projected it onto her cloth. Up and down went the needle, propelled by the nimble fingers.

"So, what's that to me?" She recognized Adrien Goyette's voice replying.

"You support the priests, Adrien! You're in their pocket! If the priests are spies then you . . ."

"Just because I attend mass doesn't put me in their pocket," Adrien interrupted. "I follow my own conscience."

The stranger lowered his tone but the words still crept into the loft.

"Alright. But what about her . . . that girl, Marie Larouche. For God's sake, man! Her father is a scout for the English army. He deserted us during the battle at Tourond's Coulee and you take her in as though she was your own daughter! At least tell her to leave."

Marie stopped sewing. She held her breath, waiting for Monsieur Goyette's reply. Sunlight slanted through the gable window and warmed her cheek, but she felt a chill of uncertainty within herself. The Goyette family were her most faithful friends, but how far would they go to protect her?

"Now you're being ridiculous!" Adrien thundered. "A fourteen year old girl is to be thrown out because her father is a scoundrel? Good heavens, when my son was captured by the English it was Marie who rescued him. She is a hero, not an outcast!"

"Nevertheless . . . " The man struggled to gain control.

"Nevertheless you are a fool to spread such gossip, Monsieur Gignac. You are new here on the Saskatchewan — it's not the same as at Fort Garry." It was Madame Goyette now. Marie smiled with relief. Nobody criticised Hélène Goyette's priests or her family and got away with it. "We go to church; we keep Marie as our daughter; and our son fights for the Métis nation. That's all there is to it — no more talk needed from you. Good day!"

Gignac was still spluttering a protest when the door slammed.

Marie resumed her work. If only she really were a Goyette. How perfect it would be to live here. If she had rescued her *brother* from the enemy camp everything would be just right. But she was not Luc's sister and that ruined it all.

The thought destroyed her concentration; she set the shirt aside and walked to the window. The Goyette farmyard lay below her. Beyond the yard a thick stand of leafless poplar trees descended a ravine that led to the river. It flowed wide and brown, still in spring flood. Luc's voice pulled her eyes back to the yard.

"I told you eh, Gignac?" He laughed, teasing the heavyset man who climbed awkwardly onto his horse. "You can't bully them."

Although he was tall for his age Luc moved with a simple grace. He carried the same confidence and sense of determination as his father but he had his mother's dark skin and her easy smile.

The man ignored Luc's taunt. "Aren't you ready yet? Hurry up!"

Luc wrapped a leather cord round the handles of a pick and shovel, then yanked the cord to pull the tools tight up against his saddle. An axe was already fastened to the other side. Luc jumped, dabbed one foot into a stirrup and landed neatly in the saddle in a single fluid motion. He looked up and waved to Marie at her window.

She felt it again. A quick surge of emotion that was affection, friendship and sympathy all mixed together. But not the love she knew he expected. She prayed his feelings would change so she wouldn't have to hurt him. Perhaps he might yet give her an easy way out.

Luc and Gignac trotted out past the barn. Luc hollered one last time and waved to his family; the sullen Gignac never glanced back.

Marie picked up her sewing. At least she had avoided a confrontation for now. Soon enough she would have to face Luc, and soon the English army would arrive. It was a bleak prospect: too bleak to think about any more. She forced the image of the wildflowers back into her mind and picked up the needle. Up and down, the orange line began moving once more.

✄ ✄ ✄

"The Dumonts couldn't shift them, so I knew *you* wouldn't," Luc said with great satisfaction. "My father may yet fight for us but it will be his choice, nobody can force him."

Gignac scowled. "How old are you boy?"

"Nearly fifteen."

Then you're old enough to shut your mouth and understand what is happening here."

He slowed his horse to a walk and Luc reined in beside him.

"I'm trying to do your family a favour. They have made themselves unpopular with Louis Riel and the Métis Provisional Government at Batoche. When the Canadian Army comes they'll follow this trail right across your farm. The soldiers will destroy it and nothing your father says will change that."

"They'll leave him alone!" Luc shot back. "He's not a rebel. He will make them see sense."

"Grow up!" Gignac barked. "You fought at Tourond's Coulee. You were a prisoner of the Canadians. Do you think they will stop to ask for permission to cross your precious farm?"

Luc remembered the lines of dead and wounded soldiers in the English camp after the battle. Gignac was right. They might take revenge on any Métis, rebel or not.

"Then where will your family go? Batoche, where they no longer have any friends? Eh?"

Rather than lose the argument, Luc nudged his horse into a canter and pulled away from Gignac. Riel, provisional governments, petitions, ultimatums . . . he didn't understand half of it. All he knew was the Canadian Army was coming to take Métis land and he was fighting to keep it.

A hawk keened its eerie call from the forest near the river. The cry echoed onto the prairie, pulling Luc's eyes to the skyline. The winged hunter was perched high on a treetop surveying his territory. Luc felt more in common with the hawk than Gignac.

A strong horse, a rifle and the freedom to roam the Saskatchewan country — that was all a young Métis man needed. Maybe later a river lot to farm and raise good horses . . . with Marie. He was certain that one day they would be together. She was so quiet lately, it was difficult to tell how she truly felt. Yet he would win her — after all, she had risked her life to help him escape the Canadian Army; she must have feelings for him.

Gignac drew abreast to repeat his question. "Well young Goyette? When the enemy come what will your stubborn father do? He'll be sorry he kept the Larouche girl then."

Luc shrugged. "I know what I'll do." He slapped his gun stock and shouted, "I'll fight as a *notinikew*. We will defeat the Canadians, just watch!"

He dug in his heels and his pony shot forward. Wind whipped his face and made him gulp.

"*Neya! Neya!*" he keened. His horse responded with a surge of speed as they left Gignac behind.

The graves were arranged in two rows. Each grave was marked by a wooden cross and each cross bore an inscription hand-carved into the wood. Six soldiers had been killed in the battle and were buried in the first row.

Tom Kerslake pulled the collar of his greatcoat up around his ears to deflect the cold wind. His uncle stood by his side. They had talked easily about the news from home. Jim had been particularly interested in Tom's letters. But now they had fallen silent. The warm May sun of the mail parade was hidden behind a stack of clouds in the western sky. The weather had changed in unison with Tom's mood. His letters, two from Violet and one from Father, had warmed him. They had reminded him how much he was loved and missed, even if they had gone a bit hysterical over the battle. Now, piling rocks on Paddy's grave to protect it from scavenging animals, he felt gray and cold.

He gazed beyond the graves toward the deep wooded ravine and the little stream that meandered through it. Fish Creek was its stupid name — it certainly wasn't big enough to have fish in it. On the other side of the coulee lay the Tourond farm — smashed and burned by cannon shells.

His eyes shifted to the second row of graves. Four more for men who had died of their wounds after the battle. Ten in all. Six were from Tom's regiment but he had not known them very well.

Then there was the final, eleventh mound with its new cross, just three days old. All that earth lay piled on top of his friend — he preferred to think about Paddy at the grassy spot on the riverbank. He read the inscription again.

RIFLEMAN PATRICK FLAHERTY
KILLED APRIL 24, 1885
AGE 19

Only it was wrong, Paddy wasn't 19. He had barely turned 18. Lied about it so the Regiment wouldn't leave him behind. Just four years older than me, Tom thought. Buglers were allowed to be fourteen for active service but not riflemen; Paddy had told the lie.

Not killed April 24th either. Why couldn't they get it right? The bushes at the edge of Fish Creek coulee had billowed a cloud of smoke when the rebels fired their first volley on April 24th. Tom could hear the thump and still see Paddy squirming on the ground, clawing at the awful red stain on his belly. Then all he remembered was lying face down in the dirt while enemy bullets rippled through the grass above him. But Paddy didn't die on April 24th.

His perpetual smile had stayed alive in the damp hospital tent for a pain-filled week. He never complained and he never despaired. Even on the last day, half full of the surgeon's laudanum, Paddy had smiled for him. Told him a silly poem.

"Hey Tommy lad. What's the date today?"

"May 1st," he answered.

"Well no work today then son," Paddy declared. His eyes were glassy and wet from fever yet still had a sparkle in them.

"Hooray, Hooray it's the first day of May.

If we get no vacation,

We'll all run away!"

Tom laughed. Paddy touched his sleeve. "Bide here, with me, Tommy. Don't leave us for a while."

That was all they had said. Tom stayed until Paddy fell asleep, then he left. They both knew Paddy would never go home to Winnipeg but Tom couldn't bring himself to say goodbye.

Anyway, May 1st was the day Rifleman Patrick
Flaherty died — not April 24th.

"Nice place really," his uncle broke the silence.
"When the leaves come out and the grass greens
it could even be pretty."

Tom couldn't see it but he didn't contradict.

"Yup, good land in this valley. Think your
father has warmed up to my idea yet? Didn't
mention it in his letter."

"Eh? What's that, Sergeant Major?" Tom
asked. "What idea?"

Jim nudged him. "We can be uncle and
nephew for a while."

"I'd like that," Tom nodded. "I've been
thinking of home since mail. What idea did you
mean?"

"Homesteading, Tom!" Jim spread his arms.
"We only talked about it twice a day on the
march from Qu'Appelle. You haven't forgotten."

"Well, I haven't thought of it since . . .
ah . . . Paddy," Tom admitted.

"The more I see, the more I like," Jim
enthused. "We could sell up at a good price in
Winnipeg and start big out here. I'd bring my
stock and the four of us with some hard work
could really make our fortunes."

"Four?" Tom grinned. "Vi thinks Winnipeg is too small. How would you get her to come out to this emptiness?"

Jim rubbed his jaw. "Well, we'd need her. We can think of something to convince her."

His uncle was an "idea man" according to Father. And Tom had been enthusiastic about homesteading before the battle, but now it didn't seem important. He didn't have the heart to say so.

"Even the three of us could do it," he said.

"That's the spirit." Uncle Jim slapped his shoulder. "Hard work and eyes on the horizon Tommy. It's the only way. No point looking back to crowded old Winnipeg. It's westward for us."

Suddenly Tom saw where the conversation was heading and he drew back from his uncle.

"Same thing applies to our lives here," Jim said seriously. "We've got a job to do. We should look forward to the end of this war. Can't look back too much."

Tom glanced away, uncomfortable. He couldn't agree to leave Paddy in the past. Yet he knew Jim was trying to help him find his answers. "Discipline and hard work." They might work for Jim, but they didn't help him with Paddy. The revenge notion though, maybe Snell of all people had something. Maybe that would answer.

"Tom!"

Walter Grayson approached, pushing a wheelbarrow full of stones. His huge red face was lit up. Corporal Snell and Alex Laidlaw followed him.

"Guess what?" he called, puffing.

"What is it, Walt?" Tom was relieved to be clear of his Uncle's advice. Jim stepped away and folded his arms — the CSM once more.

"Just met some of the boys. They said the booze finally did for old Lashbrooke. He's soused his liver once too often and it almost quit on him. He's in the hospital. We get a new Company Commander — maybe today!"

"That's Captain Lashbrooke to you, Rifleman Grayson," the Sergeant Major corrected.

"Yes, sir." Walter dumped the rocks near the grave and grinned. "Captain Lashbrooke soused himself once too often and succumbed to the booze devils."

Tom, trying to stifle a laugh, knelt to fit the stones into place on the grave mound.

"Doing a nice job, Bugler," Jim said, barely concealing his own smile. "Looks good."

Jim wished they had a few more minutes. He'd been making some progress. He felt Tom had been close to opening up — then maybe moving on from Paddy's loss. The worst were his nephew's silences; he rarely spoke of Flaherty. In fact he had hardly mentioned Paddy's name since the funeral. It didn't seem natural.

"Is it true — a new Company Commander?" Tom asked.

"Apparently so," his uncle replied. "He was scheduled to come up with the next reinforcements. Could be with that group that came in on the *Northcote* this afternoon. Let's have a look."

They paused in their work and followed him to the edge of the trail that led from the prairies down to the river. Below them the white steamboat, its name *Northcote* picked out in black letters on the bow, lay anchored. Its huge windmill paddlewheel was motionless, but a large working party streamed off her like ants. Crates of ammunition along with stacks of food and feed for the horses piled up on the shore. The reinforcements, about sixty men in scarlet tunics and navy trousers, were loading their kit into two waiting wagons.

"What about Captain Lashbrooke?" Tom asked. "Is he really so sick that he'll give up command?"

"Surgeon says he's got an infection of the liver and will have to be sent back to base hospital in Moose Jaw."

Grayson sniggered and made a drinking motion.

"We might get Lieutenant Alderson in his place." The CSM pointed to the red uniforms who were now formed into ranks and marching up from the river. "Alderson was left behind in Winnipeg sick, but if he's recovered then he should be on the steamer with these men."

The new soldiers were talking and laughing as they marched up out of the valley. A few stared at the little cemetery and several waved.

"What a rabble," Corporal Snell muttered. "They'll need some work."

One of them broke ranks and raised his rifle above his head. "Hey! What Regiment are you?"

"90th Battalion Winnipeg Rifles," Snell bellowed a little too loudly.

"Never fear, Winnipeg — the Midland Battalion is here!" The red soldier jabbed his rifle at the sky and his comrades cheered. "The heroes from Ontario will send those halfbreeds home with a bullet in their pants!"

"HEROES!" Snell's indignant sneer shot back. "THESE are our heroes!" He pointed to the crosses and the Midland cheering went silent. "Wait til a rebel spotter gets you in his sights — you'll be the ones with a bullet shoved up your . . . "

"Corporal Snell!" The CSM cut him short. "That's enough."

Snell turned away, swearing under his breath. The Midland companies marched quietly on toward the campground. A lone figure in the dark green uniform of the Winnipeg Rifles broke away from the column and approached them.

He was tall, slim to the point of being skinny and wore a sword that bounced at his side. He staggered under the weight of a large, canvas kit bag and sweat ran down his white face. He looked like someone who had recently escaped from hospital.

"Good day," he puffed cheerfully. "Do any of you . . . "

"Morning, sir," Jim snapped to attention and flourished a magnificent salute.

"Oh . . . uh . . . yes, right. Of course . . . " The young man dropped his bag and raised a scrawny hand to the brim of his glengarry cap to return the salute.

"Um . . . ," his eyes went to Jim's sleeve. "Sergeant, do you know where I might find G Company . . . uh, 90th Rifles?"

"Right here, sir, some of us anyway," Jim replied in his best soldier's voice. "I'm Company Sergeant Major Kerslake. This is Corporal Snell, Rifleman Grayson, Rifleman Laidlaw and my nephew, the company bugler, Tom Kerslake."

"Excellent. What jolly good luck." The young man made to shake hands then pulled back stiffly. "I'm ah . . . Lieutenant Alderson, just off the *Northcote*." He waved toward the steamer. "I was supposed to be second in command of G Company but I caught the measles and um . . . well here I am now. Sorry I missed the fight. Heard it was a pretty rough party, eh?"

Alex coughed; Walt pretended to be interested in the steamboat.

"Oh yes, sir. A party — a rough one, sir," Snell replied blandly. Tom turned to stare at the graves and Alderson's gaze followed. The young officer's face flushed a horrid shade of crimson. He stared at the crosses as though he'd just realized they were connected to the battle.

"Oh God, sorry men . . . um, very sorry. I didn't mean . . . party. An expression you know . . . ah, must be s-s-some of your chums over . . . there."

Jim treated Snell to one of his nasty stares. "No harm done, sir. Wasn't an easy day for us but we came through it."

An awkward silence followed, broken only by the sound of Lieutenant Alderson wheezing.

"Well, I suppose I should go report to Captain Lashbrooke," he murmured finally.

"No joy there, I'm afraid. He's very sick, an invalid," Jim explained. "You are our new Company Commander, as of today."

Alderson staggered as though he had been punched.

"Surely not!" he gasped. "But . . . ah . . . " His eyes flickered nervously back to the *Northcote*. "I've never . . . that is I'm not strictly speaking qualified for the position."

Jim picked up the kitbag easily and tossed it into the wheelbarrow. "You've got the most seniority of all the subalterns, sir." He grinned. "So you're it."

He began walking toward the cluster of tents. "If you'll follow me, I'll take you to see the battalion commander. Grayson and Laidlaw will take your kit to company headquarters."

The two men moved off and Walter trailed behind with the wheelbarrow.

"Jesus wept — we'd be better off with the Midlanders." Snell laughed harshly. "*Party* was it?"

Tom didn't reply. Paddy would have said something to make the new officer feel welcome. He glanced at Snell's hard face and somehow found it less offensive than usual. Would this new commander be the man to lead them in their fight with the rebels? Would he take them to revenge?

2
BARGAINS

No, no. It's facing the wrong angle!"
Gabriel Dumont's sturdy figure emerged
from a poplar bluff and jogged across the open
grass. His hat brim was turned up in front so the
morning sun shone full onto his face. His dark
eyes flickered everywhere, scanning the ground
and measuring the range from the trees to the St.
Antoine de Padoue Catholic Mission. The
mission consisted of a church and a two-story
rectory where the priests lived. The buildings
stood on a broad flat ridge overlooking the village
of Batoche about a kilometre away.

A second man followed Dumont from the
trees. He walked slowly, hands clasped behind his
back. His face looked up to the sun then across
toward the church. Louis Riel wore grey tweed
trousers and vest — no hat or coat — and bull-
hide moccasins. Yet he looked formal. It must

have been the thick beard, the great mass of brown hair and of course the eyes. The small piercing eyes, so bright and so searching.

"Stop digging, young Luc, and look here," Gabriel commanded.

Luc leaned on his shovel and wiped his forehead with the back of his hand — it came away slick with sweat. Dumont cradled his famous Henry repeating rifle, *Le Petit*, and pointed the barrel at the rectory.

"If the English soldiers come up the Humboldt trail past the church we want to catch them here, on the hill, in the open." He waved his arm at the grassy plateau where it dropped down into a bushy ravine. "See? Your trench faces the wrong way."

Luc saw his error and nodded but Dumont carried on discussing angles and distances. Luc's eyes were drawn to *Le Petit*'s shining brass receiver and the smooth depression where shells were fed into the magazine. Some said that Gabriel had shot ten Canadians at the Tourond Coulee fight and another four policemen at Duck Lake. It seemed fantastic that this quiet little man, patiently explaining how to dig a hole, was also the greatest Métis soldier alive.

Riel drew near and raised a hand in greeting.

"Do you understand all this talk of fortifications, young Goyette?"

"*Bonjour*, Monsieur Riel." Luc dipped his head in a miniature bow. Somehow Riel's presence seemed to demand it.

"Well?" Gabriel asked.

"Eh? Oh, yes I understand." Luc rubbed his sore hands and flicked a dribble of sweat from his eyebrow. "Then I've wasted all this time digging. Do I have to start over?"

Gabriel jumped into the pit and squatted down so his eye was level with the ground. He tossed *Le Petit* to Luc: "Here, hold this for me."

He picked up a stick and began scratching a line in the dirt leading away from the edge of the pit. He scrambled out of the trench and scurried on all fours busily scraping the line, stopping now and then to stare across the open hilltop.

"Gabriel! Such energy, like a beaver." Riel chuckled. "All these pits and trenches and ambush plans. What are you doing to this lovely place. Our beloved Batoche will be transformed into an unholy fortress."

Dumont glanced up. "Our beloved Batoche will be transformed into a police barracks if we don't defend it properly."

"God will protect us — as at Duck Lake and Tourond's. We dug no holes there. Surely once the enemy see we are resolved to defend Batoche they will agree to negotiate?"

Gabriel stopped scratching and sat back on his heels. "Louis. In all things from God I trust you with my soul. In all political negotiations I trust you with my future. But," he stabbed the stick into the earth, "to defend Batoche from English cannon you must trust me. We need to stop the soldiers here, on this ground where their shells can't reach Batoche. We need deep pits to protect our men. We nee — "

"We need faith in Jesus, Mary and Joseph," Riel interrupted. "We need prayer."

Gabriel exchanged a look of exasperation with Luc. Riel caught it and turned to Luc. "What say you? Faith or badger holes?"

"I don't know, *monsieur*. I'm only fourteen."

"Come, come. No false modesty," Riel prodded him with his intense eyes.

"Well, I think we should have raided the soldiers while they marched from Humboldt. Then they wouldn't even be here."

"Ha!" Gabriel clapped his hands. "That was my plan too."

"Precisely, Gabriel." Riel continued to stare at Luc. "That was your idea — not his. Let us hear your thoughts, Luc."

Luc gathered his nerve and plunged forward. "Since they are here then we must entrench. Their cannon shells will knock us flat if we don't go underground. But my mother says we should not be fighting at all. She says God will decide who governs here, and I agree with her too."

"Come on, Louis," Gabriel scolded. "He's a boy. This is between you and me."

Riel's eyes left Luc and travelled to Dumont. "But the church. Trenches in the churchyard? Fighting in God's house?"

"It's you who denounced the priests and the church, Louis! Why only yesterday . . . "

Luc lifted the rifle and squinted down the sights, lining them up on a tree trunk. The argument was pointless; the soldiers were here and the Métis had to fight. There was no use debating it over and over. What a rifle — a real Métis man's weapon. His old shotgun was nothing compared to this. He loved the feel of the polished stock in his palm.

"On this, Louis, I will not budge. We must get back to work." Gabriel stood up and Luc reluctantly returned *Le Petit* to him.

"There, see now?" Gabriel asked. "Just extend your trench this way and you will be able to shoot in both directions. It might prove useful."

Luc nodded and reached for his shovel with a sigh. "We have dug more pits than we have men to fill them," he grumbled.

Dumont laughed. "You fought well at Tourond's, Luc. You're one of my best soldiers but you still have a lot to learn. Those holes will be as important as our rifles when the English come, so keep digging."

A horse and rider appeared around the corner of the rectory.

"Well, well. Here's one I'd given up on," Riel said warily. "You talk to him Gabriel. This will not be my type of negotiation."

It was Luc's father.

Luc's fist tightened on the shovel and his heart began to pound. Hope and fear raced alternately through him. Had Father finally come to join them? Or was this a confrontation to force him to choose between his family and the rebellion? He had searched within himself many times and never found an answer. He did not know where his loyalty truly lay and there was no simple solution.

"Adrien!" Dumont called pleasantly, shifting his rifle so that the butt rested on his right hip. "You've come to join our army? Better late than never, eh?" He laughed but there was no humour in his tone.

"Gabriel . . . please, no trouble," Luc whispered. Dumont half turned and Luc was startled at the transformation. Only a minute ago Gabriel's face had been placid and kind as he patiently explained about the trench. But now the eyes were like tiny black fires and the muscles in his jaw flexed, tense and hard. The peaceful lamb had become a lean wolf in the twinkling of an eye. *Le Petit*'s muzzle lowered ever so slowly until it covered Adrien Goyette.

Luc shivered. The sweat on his brow was suddenly an icy damp. The rifle he had just admired now repulsed him; he felt sick.

"Dumont," Adrien nodded as he pulled up before them. He deliberately failed to acknowledge

Riel's presence. "Good luck for me; I've come to speak to both you and Luc."

The repeating rifle quivered slightly but remained targeted on Adrien.

"Luc is *my* soldier," Gabriel snapped. "You speak to me — his captain."

Luc drew a sharp breath and held it, afraid to even breathe. Adrien's face flushed red.

"How dare you!" He pulled back hard and the horse reared up then came down, hooves slamming into the earth near Dumont.

"He's my SON! I'll speak to him whenever I . . ."

Dumont leaped away from the plunging horse, worked the lever on his rifle to jack a shell into the chamber and brought the gun up to his shoulder in one quick motion.

"WATCH YOURSELF, GOYETTE!"

"And you, DUMONT!" Adrien savagely reined his horse sideways toward Gabriel.

"*NON! Arrête,*" Luc bellowed. He grabbed the horse's bit, pulling its head down. He kept his back squarely in front of *Le Petit* while he pushed the frightened animal back a few paces. Then he turned to look for Riel as a peacemaker. Why wasn't he helping? Riel stared intently at the church — was he praying? He did not even see the violence about to erupt.

The horse snorted, shook its head and stood still. A chickadee shrilled from the trees near the rectory as though scolding them: *chick-a-dee-dee.*

Gabriel lowered his rifle slightly.

Then quiet.

Both men stared fiercely at each other and Luc breathed deeply to control his shaking hands. It was up to him now, whether he liked it or not.

"Have you come to take me home, Father?" He spoke quietly, trying to sound calm. "Because if you have — "

"No," Adrien said, cutting him short.

"No?" Gabriel repeated. "You haven't come to force Luc to quit?"

Adrien shook his head. "You've gone off half-cocked as usual Dumont, picking a fight where none was intended."

Gabriel set his rifle butt on the ground and the anger seemed to flow out of him. "Well," he shrugged. "You're hardly a friend of the Métis cause; what was I supposed to think?"

"That's your trouble, you don't think. You and Riel drag us into this insane rebellion without a thought of the consequences."

"Father, please," Luc said. "No lectures. Its too late for that."

"True enough," his father conceded. "Anyway its food I've come to see you about — not the Métis nation."

"Talk food, Gabriel," Riel prompted. "We do need food. I will see you at Letendre's." He turned and walked back toward Batoche.

Adrien swung down off the horse and passed the lines to Luc. Then he pulled his pipe from his coat pocket and stuffed it full of tobacco. Dumont stepped forward with a match and in return Adrien offered his tobacco pouch. Luc sagged with relief. The little act of lighting their pipes said more than any words of apology. No Métis would share a pipe with an enemy he intended to fight. Tobacco smoke billowed as both men puffed vigorously. Luc savoured the rich scent.

"Food is what your men — not to mention the women and children in the village — will need if the Canadians lay siege to you here." Adrien pointed his pipe stem down the hill to the cluster of buildings in the distance.

Gabriel nodded. "Food, ammunition, rifles," he paused to wink at Adrien. "And soldiers. We need more experienced soldiers, like you."

Adrien ignored the joke.

"I suppose you have a plan to feed us?" Dumont said.

"Six bags of good flour made from Goyette wheat — each a hundred weight. Six hundred pounds of flour in total."

"Never!" Gabriel exclaimed. "Where? We've been to your farm and there was no six hundred weight of flour there. Where is it hidden?"

"First my terms, then I'll tell you where," Adrien said carefully. "You let me move four bags to sell and I'll give you the other two for free."

"Ha! I'll confiscate all six right now," Gabriel cried. "The Provisional Council can pay you later."

"You can't take it if you don't know where it is," Adrien pointed out. "Two for you and four for me to market, or nothing for anybody."

Dumont puffed his pipe, eyes gazing far away as he calculated the problem. "Three for us and three for you to sell," he offered. "We have so many to feed."

"Alright, but I must take Luc to help me move it," Adrien countered.

"A deal." Dumont stuck out his hand and they shook. "Now where is it hidden?"

"In the shed behind your own store," Adrien said.

"MY STORE! At the crossing?" Dumont squawked in disbelief.

"Oh yes. I left it there a month ago, remember? Hillyard Mitchell was supposed to pick it up but your ferry wasn't working and you said . . . "

Gabriel cut in. "I said leave it in the shed until he could get it." He stomped his foot in anger. "All that food on my own farm, right under my nose. You tricked me, Goyette, my God . . . "

"But you have made a bargain," Luc spoke up.

Dumont whipped his hat off and smacked it against his thigh.

"Well, if we leave now," Adrien said briskly, "we can have it back here before night."

Dumont hesitated for a moment then smiled. "You always were the crafty one, Goyette. Go now and bring us our flour — three bags remember."

G Company was just about the best-drilled company in the whole battalion, Tom thought smugly.

"Cumpny Right In . . . CLINE!" The Sergeant Major bellowed and two long parallel lines of green-jacketed soldiers pivoted smartly to the right.

"At the trail, on the double, foooorm . . . LINE!"

The soldiers deftly lifted their rifles, jogged in a wide sweeping turn and came to a halt in two perfectly reformed lines facing at right angles from their first position.

From his place beside the right marker, Tom could feel the pride that held them tightly in their ranks, alert and poised. Perhaps the best-drilled company in the entire army.

"G Company. Present . . . ARMS!" The command brought their rifles up in a salute.

Lieutenant Alderson marched awkwardly to the Sergeant Major. Uncle Jim saluted smartly and engaged the young man in a murmured conversation.

Alderson's immaculate green and black uniform, shiny new boots and gleaming sword belt contrasted with the faded, patched and fraying uniforms that the rest of the company wore. He was pale, soft and skinny while they were brown, hard and lean. But then they had marched two hundred miles through the spring mud. They had slept rough and unwashed for days on end. They had fought the rebel army in the tangled bush at Fish Creek. And Lieutenant Alderson had not. He needed to gain their confidence. He needed to show himself to be confident and competent. And in the two days since he had stepped off the *Northcote*, Lieutenant Alderson had been neither confident nor competent.

"Oh what a thrill, Napoleon has arrived." A loud whisper from the ranks. Tom glanced back at Snell. The men sniggered. Admittedly Alderson was terribly inexperienced and not very good at drill, but what could you expect after only a couple of days? Tom felt a protective instinct towards the gawky young officer. Yet he knew the others were probably right. If they were to go into battle again surely this boy could not be relied on to lead them.

"Right men, ah . . . your attention please?" Alderson's voice was a deep baritone but that seemed to accentuate its nervous flutter. The CSM marched to his place behind the rear rank.

"This morning we will be practising the advance to contact, skirmishing by half company, and the attack."

He pointed at a large patch of willows about three hundred metres away. "Those bushes will represent the enemy position which we . . . uh, will of course . . . um, attack."

He paused, as though uncertain of what to say next.

"I suppose we should . . . ah, no, perhaps not."

Another silence mired him down and he whirled around rapidly to face the willows.

"At this rate," Snell's hoarse whisper again, "even the bushes will defeat us." It earned him a growl from the Sergeant Major and sent a ripple of laughter down the ranks.

Tom squirmed with embarrassment. Why couldn't Alderson just spit it out. The men were accustomed to loud, clear orders. *Just DO something!* he felt like yelling at the frozen young officer. He looked so terribly lonely, forced to stand before them, solitary and exposed to their ridicule. He needed somebody by his side.

"Um . . . Bugler, to Me!" Alderson called, as though reading his mind. Tom wrenched himself from the front rank and jogged to the lieutenant.

Sweat poured down Alderson's face even though it was a cool morning. His Adam's apple ploughed rapidly up and down as though he had to gulp for each breath.

He returned Tom's salute then suddenly drew his sword with a wild flourish that caused Tom to dodge back a step for fear of being sliced.

"G Company will advance. Quick . . . ah . . . march!" He began striding forward, sword held rigidly at arm's length, aimed at the clump of willows.

"No!" Tom blurted out. "Sir, you can't go yet. The men are still presenting arms — they can't move."

Alderson's face burned a bright pink and his eyes bulged as he twirled around to stare at the motionless soldiers. Another long hush descended as he replaced his sword in its scabbard. Most of the men were grinning and Walter Grayson's big belly was bouncing with suppressed laughter. Just when Tom thought the whole drill would have to be cancelled, the young officer managed to produce the correct commands. G Company began its advance.

Tom tucked his bugle under his arm and glanced back at the company. The front rank followed close behind. The men were spaced about a metre apart and carried their rifles waist high so that they were ready for action. The second rank, shepherded by his uncle, followed at a forty metre interval. When they were about halfway to the "enemy" bushes, Alderson gave the order to halt.

"At this point we will assume that rebels hidden in the bushes have opened fire on us," he said, turning to face the men. "So we have made contact with the . . . ah . . . with the . . . um . . . enemy."

Keep going! Tom urged him mentally. *Don't stop to explain — just give the orders.* But it was too late. The sight of all those men demanding his leadership, staring, waiting, was too much. His sword drooped. He began gulping for air again. This time he was sunk. G Company was past ridicule. They no longer saw their commander as a cartoon — he was an embarrassing liability.

"YOU heard the Lieutenant!" Uncle Jim's indignant roar jolted them. "You're under fire — commence skirmish drills!"

The rear rank instantly lay down. The front rank knelt like a string of hunting dogs on point. They began to simulate the loading and firing of their rifles. Tom tugged Alderson's sleeve and led him to the left end of the front rank.

"Our position is here, sir," he said quietly. "You direct the — "

"Yes, I know," Alderson replied. "I direct the skirmishers' fire, assess the enemy strength, then order a company advance if I judge it necessary."

Tom's surprise was plain on his face. The young officer drew a deep breath.

"D-darn it Bugler! I know WHAT to do. I just c-c-c-can't get the words out. Blast this stutter and blast me to hell for a nervous m-m-milque-toast."

"You can't expect to command this company if you stutter!"

Tom said it and immediately wished the words back in his mouth. They struck Alderson hard.

"CEASEFIRE!" Alderson screamed, furious that his secret was out and suddenly reckless because of it.

"Rear rank, CLOSE!"

The men, startled by the unexpected force of the orders, did as they were told. The rear rank ran up to form behind the front rank and the entire company stood ready. Alderson looked more surprised than anyone. His anger faded and the terror seemed to creep back into him.

Tom grabbed his own bayonet, pulling it partially clear of the scabbard and coughed loudly. Alderson took the hint. He moved to his place in front of the company.

"Company! Fix B . . . ah, Fix B . . . B . . . ," his voice quavered and he squeezed his eyes shut. "BAYONETS."

The long sword-knives snapped onto the rifle muzzles, forming a glittering line of sharp steel. The rapid metallic clicking sent a shiver down Tom's spine. An infantry bayonet assault — the last desperate act in battle. They had attacked like this at Fish Creek into close-range rebel gunfire that had broken the charge into fragments.

"Ch . . . ch . . . ," Alderson's eyes found Tom. They pleaded for help. He had no power left to defeat the stutter. Tom whipped the bugle to his lips and played the high repetitive notes that drew G Company forward cheering and yelling. Lieutenant Alderson waved his sword and galloped like an ungainly colt. Tom felt the officer's relief that the time for commands was over. He could just run at the head of his men.

Tom's horn seemed to understand because it came alive in his hands, calling the Winnipeg Riflemen to attack.

Then the young officer's sword scabbard slipped off his belt hook and fell; the tip swung between his legs and in a flash his feet were tripped out from under him. He flew headfirst into the deep grass. Tom had a glimpse of the sword flying free and Alderson's hat jamming over his eyes as his face ploughed into the earth. Tom and G Company never hesitated. They swept onward and swamped the "enemy" willow bushes, leaving their commander in a tangled heap behind them.

3
SCOUTS AT THE
CROSSING

Gabriel's Crossing was ten kilometres up the river from Batoche. Luc and his father arrived in their wagon just before noon.

"Hold them here." Adrien pulled the team to a halt and passed the lines to Luc. They were at the top of a long slope that dropped down to river level where a small cluster of buildings sat close to the water's edge. A cable stretched across the river from the buildings to the far shore. The square wooden barge that was Gabriel's ferry lay beached nearby.

Adrien walked partway down the slope then stopped to examine the Crossing. A moment later he waved Luc forward.

"Just wanted to make certain the English weren't here ahead of us," he explained as he climbed back into the wagon.

"Gabriel has our men watching the main trails," Luc said. He let the horses take their own pace slowly down the hill. "He would have told us if there was danger."

"True enough, but it doesn't hurt to see for yourself."

Luc didn't argue. He'd never get his father to trust Gabriel and it was pointless to bicker over it.

The flour was stacked at the back of the shed under a canvas tarpaulin. Using short, shuffling steps they hoisted each bag out to the wagon.

"We'll drop our three at home and take the other three on to Batoche after we've had something to eat," Adrien announced as the last sack thumped onto the wagon bed in a cloud of white dust.

Luc rested his back on the box, panting from the heavy work. "Do you think we could take a short rest . . . maybe play a game of billiards before we go?"

"Why not?" Adrien smiled. They walked to the front of Dumont's small store. It really wasn't much of a store — just a few bits of merchandise and tackle — but it did have a slate bed billiard table with fine green cloth and a polished wood frame.

Luc's conscience was disturbed by his father's simple act of friendship. How could he defy Father and fight for Riel? Three hundred pounds of food freely given in an act of charity and what thanks did he get? A cocked rifle with threats from Gabriel, and disobedience from his own son.

Adrien paused at the door. "Something wrong?"

Luc avoided his father's eyes and studied the ridge line to the south. "Not really. I was wondering . . . " The Métis cause seemed far away. Right now he was happy just to be enjoying a day with Father. Suddenly he missed his little brother and sister — felt a surge of homesickness and envisioned his mother worrying about him. Then there was Marie and a fresh pang of regret struck him.

"I wondered if maybe I should come home, for a while. You need help on the farm. And I'm the one who brought Marie to stay; I should try to take better care of her."

"What a notion!" Father laughed. "Marie takes care of us! And she does at least as much work as you ever did."

"Hey!" Luc gave his father a friendly punch on the arm. "I work hard, you know. Look at these calluses."

"Luc," Adrien's fingers touched him lightly. "I don't agree with Riel and I would like nothing better than for you to come home. You've fought well for them so you don't owe them anything. But it's your choice now; I can't force you."

Father's voice seemed to catch on something and he coughed. "You must do what you think is right."

For once Luc's rebellious instincts were quiet. He wished somebody could make the decision for him. An urge to quit the fighting and go home tugged powerfully. Only his pride stood fast in the way.

"Mother of God!" Adrien cried. "Back to the shed. *Vite, Vite.* The Canadians are here!"

The south ridge, empty seconds earlier, was now topped by a half dozen riders. They were well spread out and approached at a cautious walk. Even at four-hundred metres distance their rifles were easily visible, balanced across their saddles.

"Did they see us?" Luc asked, crouching behind the back wall.

Adrien lay on the ground and peered around the corner. "No, I don't think so. They're moving slowly and they're calm."

Fear grabbed Luc's stomach and twisted it. The old terror from Tourond's Coulee crept back into him.

"Six, no wait . . . another six behind them," Father whispered hoarsely. "Twelve men but only one wears a uniform. Do you know who they are?"

Luc swallowed to control his voice but it quavered anyway. "Is that one wearing a red coat and white helmet?"

"Yes."

"Boulton's Scouts," he croaked, "*éclaireurs*. Their best men. Good horsemen, good shots. They'll catch us for sure." He looked wildly to the wagon. "Or shoot us. We have to run."

"Wait," Adrien commanded. "We'll never make it back up that hill with six-hundred pounds of flour in the wagon. They'll chase us down in no time. Let me think."

Luc stood trembling, his mind filled with the desire to flee right now without thinking.

"I've got an idea. Come on." Father ran to the wagon and pushed Luc toward the horses. "Hold them still. The soldiers can't see us yet. We're hidden by the store so we're safe here for a minute."

He whipped his knife from its sheath and deftly cut the traces, freeing the horses from the wagon. Then he reached under the seat, retrieved the shotgun and tossed it to Luc. Nervous hands fumbled it — Luc had to snatch at the gun twice to get a solid grip on it. One of the horses whinnied. Luc cringed at the noise but held the reins tight.

Adrien appeared from the back of the wagon staggering under a flour bag. He flung it across one horse, just forward of the collar. The horse snorted and skittered sideways.

"Hold him Luc!"

Luc could do nothing else. A fearful paralysis had replaced his urge to run.

"Flour?" he bleated, looking over his shoulder, imagining how close the scouts must be. "Shouldn't we just leave it?"

"The day I leave all my food and run from a bunch of English farmers . . . ," Adrien grunted as he threw a second bag up behind the first one, " . . . will never come." He tied the flour down with a piece of rope. "There, at least we've saved two hundreds. Now follow me quietly."

He led one horse and Luc followed with the other toward the river. They were careful to stay in the shadow of the store and shed.

"See where the trees grow near the river?" Adrien pointed to the spot. "A trail starts just there. We can follow it uphill through the woods and reach the main road near the top. Then we mount and make a dash over the crest. If God is kind, we'll be gone before these soldiers even have a chance to see us." He cackled, almost as though he was enjoying himself.

The hill was steep and the path narrow but Luc's nervous energy carried him up it easily. They stopped near the top and Adrien climbed onto the spare horse. Luc mounted behind him and wrapped one arm tightly around Father's waist; the other hand gripped the shotgun. His knees clamped the horse. It warmed his legs and the familiar smell calmed him. Now that they were mounted — even doubled up — he felt more confident of their escape.

Adrien looked back and made the sign of the cross. "Ready? We go fast now, so hang on."

He kicked the horse into a trot, jerked the packhorse's reins and it swung into place behind them. A flurry of branches slapped at them, tugging at their clothes, stinging like spring mosquitoes. They burst clear of the bush onto the road. The crest of the hill lay a few metres above them.

Luc swivelled with a surge of fear, expecting to see Boulton's men, but the road was empty. The enemy scouts were distant tiny figures far below, just dismounting at Gabriel's store.

"We did it!" He laughed with relief. "We fooled the *éclaireurs*."

They reached the top and Adrien nudged the horses into a canter. Luc relaxed his grip and slouched back, bouncing in easy rhythm with the horse's rocking motion. The trees thinned as they approached the open prairie and he caught sight of the river below. Father slowed the horse back to a walk. They were completely hidden from the Crossing; nothing could touch them now.

"HOLD THERE! STAND FAST!"

Three horses grazed beside the trail, only a few metres away. Two men sat in the tall grass smoking, a third was climbing to his feet and pointing at them. Wide-brimmed hats with red bandannas wrapped round the crown. Winchester repeating rifles in the saddle rings. Weathered brown faces with long whiskers and sharp eyes. Boulton's Scouts.

Luc saw and understood. The cutoff men. They must have circled in from the east prairie ahead of the main body to block the trail. No escape now.

Adrien's heels kicked back savagely and their horse leaped into a clumsy, frightened gallop. It seemed to run out from under Luc. He grabbed desperately at father's shirt but couldn't stop from sliding sideways off the horse's bare back. The shotgun clutched in his right hand thudded against Adrien's ribs and lodged under his armpit. Luc's left leg thrashed wildly under the horse's belly while his right leg pointed straight up over its heaving hindquarters.

He dangled nearly upside down, helpless as a fish on a hook. He had a brief glimpse of the men scrambling for their rifles before thick dust filled his eyes and mouth.

Adrien's hand appeared through the haze and grasped his collar. With one mighty heave he pulled Luc upright. Luc coughed and spat a lump of dirt from the back of his throat. Then they both leaned forward and bent low beside the horse's neck trying to make as small a target as possible. The hair on Luc's neck prickled and a horrible shiver went down his spine — waiting for the bullet that must come.

CRACK

The scout's slug buzzed over their heads. Adrien kicked frantically at their horse but it was a heavy working animal and had no real speed.

"You're too high!" roared an English voice. "Shoot for the horse!"

Another shot. The pack horse screamed and surged forward to draw even with them. Blood streamed from its flank where the bullet had gouged a long furrow. Its eyes bulged wild and white with terror. It lurched sideways and the heavy body slammed into Luc's leg. He felt their own horse veer off at a crazy angle. He lifted his knee and kicked at the wounded animal. His foot skidded across its torn flesh spattering crimson droplets over his moccasin. The wounded horse leaped away from them and Adrien dropped its reins. Then two more shots came in quick succession but they went wide.

A large poplar bluff stood two hundred metres ahead of them. The trail turned sharply into the trees. Luc glanced over his shoulder and was surprised at how far they had come. Two scouts had given up shooting and were running for their horses. The third one was kneeling to take careful aim. Luc stared in fascinated horror at the rifle's muzzle. It puffed a small cloud of smoke and he instinctively ducked his head. The bullet slapped beside his ear and a small rip opened magically in Father's shirt, high up on his shoulder.

"*Mon Dieu!*" Adrien gasped.

A red stain spread slowly through the cloth only inches from Luc's eyes. Father was shot. He couldn't tear his eyes away from the oozing bullet hole. The English scouts had shot his father, that was all he could comprehend. No fear, no pity, just that one astonished thought lodged in his brain.

"Luc," Adrien called over the thumping hoof-beats. "Is it bad?"

"I . . . I don't know." Luc tried to think — concentrate on the wound. Dark blood, not crimson. Leaking from the hole, not pumping. Was that good? "It's bleeding," he said.

"Did it hit any bones?"

"I can't tell."

"Well for God's sake," Father snapped impatiently. "Feel my shoulder and find out!"

Luc inched his free hand up and poked Adrien's shoulder blade — then his collar bone. They were rigid.

"No," he yelled. "Father? I think it missed your — "

"Alright that's good. I have a plan for when we reach the trees."

The bluff was now only a few metres away. Adrien pulled back on the horse to slow it for the sharp turn into the woods.

"We can't outrun them riding double. Once we're in the bush you jump down and hide. I'll lead them up the road. After they've gone past, you can go down to the river and follow it home."

"No!" The image of his unarmed father being ridden down by the ruthless scouts was unbearable. "I can't just hide while you sacrifice yourself."

"I'm not asking your opinion!" Father bellowed. "Do as I say now or we'll both be taken."

They passed the first trees and curved right until the pursuing soldiers were out of sight. Adrien reined back hard and the frightened animal slewed sideways to a prancing halt. He swung his good arm back and knocked Luc off the horse.

"Go!" he shouted. "Go, boy, and hide!"

Luc scrambled to his feet and for a split second caught his father's eyes. They were sad.

"God be with you, my son."

Then horse and rider were gone, pounding down the trail.

Luc darted off the road and rolled into a chokecherry bush. Not enough cover. He crawled behind a thick tangle of willow and lay flat. Only a minute ago they had been safe and laughing. Now he burrowed like a frightened rabbit while his father, already wounded, was about to be hunted down. The sound of running horses reached him. The scouts had mounted and were on their way. There was no time to consider the situation. He had two choices: stop them or let them go by. Save his father or let him be killed.

He broke the shotgun open and checked both barrels. They were clean, and each contained a shell charged with heavy buckshot. He snapped it shut, forcing himself to ignore his fear. He had to think clearly. Two shots from his gun should take the scouts by surprise, forcing them to dismount. They would try to manoeuvre around behind him but that would take time — time enough for father to get away. The only problem was his own escape. How would he get past the scouts to the river without being seen?

A whitetail deer gave him the answer. It was a doe. Startled by the approaching horses, she flew down the road past him, then cut into the trees. Her white flag waved gaily, beckoning him to follow her as she bounced almost silently through the thick bush. Luc ran after her and found a well-trodden game trail leading down a shallow ravine. Her dancing white tail vanished where the trail dropped to the river.

"*Merci mon Dieu, merci,*" Luc whispered. God must have sent that doe to rescue him. By His grace, Luc knew he now had a chance. A half-fallen, dead tree lay at the junction of the deer trail and the road. A perfect spot to spring his ambush.

"SLOW UP! Watch yourselves."

The English voice came from just beyond the forest. Luc flopped down behind the broken tree and thrust his shotgun through the branches. He cocked both hammers and pulled the butt tight to his shoulder. Taking a huge breath, he then blew it out slowly to steady himself as he squinted down the barrels. The gunsight was a tiny brass bead on the muzzle. It was aimed just above an opening in the trees where the road turned in. Perfect.

The riders suddenly appeared in the opening. The first one flashed by before Luc could fire. The drumming hooves sent a jolt of panic down his finger and it jerked the first trigger.

BOOM

Smoke billowed and Luc's buckshot whipped harmlessly through the branches above the trail.

"Hell's fire!" Luc roared in frustration and quickly resighted. The second rider made a mistake. He reined in at the sound of the shot and stopped still, centred in the clearing. Luc's heartbeat thumped in his ears and for an instant everything seemed to freeze. The scout's curious face, brown and whiskered, stared intently down the road. His horse stood rigid, all four legs locked immobile. The brass bead sight hovered on the soldier's leg where his corduroy trousers were stuffed into the leather boot top.

"*Ay Ay Mawinewhew!*" Luc's Cree warrior spirit screamed, breaking the spell. He yanked the trigger and the second barrel exploded.

The horse reared, staggering on its haunches. The Englishman's hat spun into the air and he clutched his leg as he slid from the saddle. The third scout leaped from his horse, diving for cover.

But Luc didn't wait to see anymore. He began crawling like a crazed earthworm, nose in the dirt, elbows and knees wriggling his body down the deer path.

"Take cover! Where are they? Are you hurt? Over here, over here! Not too bad, my leg."

A confusion of English shouts echoed through the trees. Luc kept his head down and ploughed forward, cradling the shotgun in his hands like a baby.

"Let go o' yer horse Billy! Git! Git!"

The sound of hoofbeats again, only this time leaving the trees. Luc smiled. They were sending their horses out of danger rather than risk losing them. Only now they'd never remount in time to catch Father.

He reached the point where the path was sheltered by the small ravine and then he climbed to his feet and began running, crouched over, without a backward glance. Soon the gully widened and dropped steeply. His feet felt like they were churning high up past his head as he flew down the bank in huge, lunging strides. He flailed his free arm to keep his balance and went even faster. The track flattened, the trees disappeared and river water flowed not five metres away. His left foot smashed into a rock and he fell full length on the shore.

He lay still, gasping for air, then giggling with relief. The smooth, firm mud was a cool delight against his cheek. English voices called but they were too far away to be understood. Luc stood up, scraping mud from his face and clothes. Then he picked up his shotgun and began jogging along the river toward home.

4
INTO THE RECTORY

Major Boulton's Mounted Infantry — the Scouts — rode four abreast in a column led by General Middleton. The General's tubby body and long white moustache were easy to spot, even at a long distance.

"They look good; they know what they're doing," said Lieutenant Alderson enviously.

"They *are* good," Tom agreed. The column of horsemen snaked across the prairie toward camp. "Uncle Jim says they're the best scouts he's seen."

"Lucky beggars," Alderson said softly. "Scouts have no need of drill. No open orders, inclines or echelons. No bayonets to forget either."

Tom heard the self-criticism in Alderson's voice but what could he, as bugler, say to his officer without sounding insubordinate. He tried to think of something positive.

"Well, you recognized the bugle calls and Uncle Jim says you can recite your drill commands perfectly so with a little more practice . . . "

Alderson stiffened. "So, Sergeant Major Kerslake discusses my shortcomings with Bugler Kerslake behind my back, does he?"

Tom flushed; he should have kept his mouth shut. Now he'd insulted the man.

"I suppose your uncle resents my command. He's probably happy to see me fumble my orders."

"No, sir. You are wrong there." Tom looked Alderson in the eye. "The Sergeant Major would NEVER do that. He says discipline is the only thing that wins battles and all soldiers are bound to follow orders no matter ho . . . uh . . . "

Tom stopped as he realized he was just about to insult the young officer again. When would he learn to keep his mouth shut? Alderson returned Tom's stare for a long, uncomfortable moment; then he burst into laughter.

"Oh for pity's sake, stand easy, Bugler Kerslake! I know the truth — you don't have to sugar-coat it. I can recite all my orders perfectly from the drill manual." He sighed. "But it's another thing standing alone, front and centre, trying to command men who have actually fought the rebels while I was cruising comfortably up the river on a steamboat."

He looked away, studying the scouts. "Well, it's deuced difficult you see. It's as though I'm an ignorant child and you're all real soldiers."

This time Tom did keep quiet. Alderson shouldn't be revealing all these inner secrets to his bugler. He would resent pity and pity was all Tom felt.

"Still, mustn't bleat, eh? More practice and I will get better." He turned back. "You're quite the prickly one aren't you, Kerslake? Thought for a moment there you were going to 'offer violence to a superior'!"

Tom fiddled self-consciously with his bugle.

"I suppose that shouldn't surprise me, though. I've heard a lot about your bravery during the battle."

A familiar stab of guilt struck Tom, as it did whenever somebody mentioned his heroics at Fish Creek.

"Ah, people exaggerate, sir."

"Come now, no false modesty," Alderson smiled kindly. "Two charges — saved Corporal Snell's life — captured a rebel. Those are the facts as I understand it."

"And left my best friend dying because I was too frightened to go to his help. Hiding my nose in the weeds while Paddy lay gutshot, crying for his mother."

The words tumbled out like a summer cloudburst. One second bright sunlight — the next, torrents of rain.

"Well, this seems to be the afternoon for confessing our hidden fears," Alderson said. "I'm certain you're not to blame for Flaherty; you couldn't have saved his life."

"No I couldn't," Tom agreed. "But that doesn't make it feel any better."

They fell silent as Boulton's men drew near.

"You there, 90th!" The General's aide left the column and galloped up to them. Alderson came to attention and saluted. "At your service, sir."

"Right, Lieutenant," the aide returned the salute. "We had a brush with the rebels at Gabriel's Crossing, got one man wounded. Fetch Doctor Ralston and a couple of stretcher bearers. Then tell the brigade surgeon he's got a customer."

Two scouts helped a third slide down sideways from his horse. He was pale, and blood smeared his hands where he clutched his left leg. His boot was gone and a rough, red-stained bandage was wrapped around his knee.

"Doesn't look too bad," Tom said. He had seen the same or much worse forty times over during the battle. "Unless the knee is smashed of course — then he'll be crippled."

Alderson hid his surprise at seeing the injured man. It seemed so unreal. While he and young Tom had been practising bugle calls, these men had been shooting it out with rebels. Yet nobody seemed the least bit concerned — even the casualty who now lay on the ground, propped up on one elbow, loading tobacco into his pipe.

"Looks bad enough to me," Alderson said as they turned to go find the doctors.

"Could be worse, sir," Tom said sadly. "Could be dying slow and painfully from a bullet in the belly."

Alderson glanced at his young companion. The glengarry cap was set low over the bugler's forehead and his hard eyes showed no sympathy for the wounded scout. A tough little man — yet also a boy who seemed to be hurting badly inside.

"Marguerite, NO!" Madame Goyette brushed the little girl away from the table. "Marie . . . please."

Marie took Jerome and Marguerite by their hands and drew them back.

"Let go, I want to help Papa!"

Marie knelt beside Marguerite and put her arms around her shoulders. "Mama will make him better, don't worry. We can best help if we don't get in her way."

The child seemed to accept this and fell silent. Madame Goyette's quick brown hands had already cleaned the wound; the bleeding had nearly stopped. She folded a bandage torn from a strip of clean linen.

"Thank God," she murmured. "A bit lower and you might have lost your arm." The bullet had dug a shallow groove through the flesh at the top of his shoulder. "You were lucky. We must say a special prayer of thanks. Maybe Father Moulin will offer it on our behalf at mass."

She spoke as calmly as if she had been washing a potato for supper rather than a bullet wound in her husband. But her face was stiff with worry.

"Moulin? I'd rather Father Fourmond spoke for us," Adrien said. "When you're finished I'll take the pony and go up the river to meet Luc."

"Yes, I'll be done in a minute." Hélène rapped him lightly with her finger. "And please show more respect for Father Moulin."

Marie listened tensely — how could they be so calm? Madame Goyette's dark face and heavy black braids reflected her Cree mother but it was her Métis father that had taught her to be a Christian. She was well known for her powerful faith and devotion to the Catholic church. She could face any calamity with that faith and throw in the right prayer as well. But her own husband had been shot; their son was out there alone; a wagon and a horse were lost; soldiers coming at any second . . .

"Marie!" Marguerite yelped. "That hurts, let go!"

Marie relaxed her grip on the little girl's hand.

"If the English soldiers come while you're gone, what should we say?" she asked.

Adrien shook his head. "They won't come this far; they were a scouting party. I lost them miles back."

"You old fox. No policeman could catch my *notinikew* — even on a plough horse," Hélène proudly declared. Adrien laughed at her compliment.

"I doubt they went much farther than the woods where I left Luc."

Suddenly both parents fell silent. Had the scouts found Luc? Was he a prisoner, or worse? Marie tried to keep the fear at bay. Métis people on the Saskatchewan were accustomed to hardship and danger. If Luc's mother could be so strong then she would — she must — be strong as well. She fingered the tiny silver figure of the Virgin Mary that hung from her neck on a heavy thread.

It was no use. The thought of Luc injured, captured or dead . . . it was too much to bear. His face, his laugh and his eyes appeared before her and she ached to see him again, to know he was safe. The image of Luc also brought guilt. He loved her but she hadn't returned it. Now that he might be gone she was wallowing in pity for her own feelings — for her loss. Tears stung and she wiped them away. Be strong! What was love anyway? Did Luc really know? How could she tell?

"Hello in there!" A voice called to them. *Luc? Could it be?* "Anybody at home?"

Marie was the first one out the door. She raced across the farmyard toward the boy and horse that appeared from the trees near the river. It *was* Luc. She saw the smile she had just prayed for and a contented warmth tingled through her. It was more than relief; it was as though she had wished him to be born again and he had been. Then she was hugging him, crushing him, and tears flowed to accompany her sobs.

"Marie," he whispered, holding her tightly. His lips brushed her cheek. "Don't cry — I'm safe. I have come back to you."

One part of her mind rebelled at the kiss. Did she want him, really? Or was it just fear that he'd been killed. She mustn't mislead him or hurt him. She should pull back until she was certain of her feelings but she couldn't let him go. Nor could she stop crying. What was wrong with her?

"My son!" Madame Goyette arrived and wrestled Luc from her grip. Marie saw the Mother's love in her face. "Merciful God, thank you for bringing my boy back to me."

"Did Father get home? Is he safe?"

"Oh yes," Hélène laughed. "The crazy man, risking his life for two bags of flour."

Suddenly Marie felt foolish and stepped back in confused embarrassment. She dried her face and turned away.

"Look what I found, Mama," Luc said proudly. He pulled the horse forward. It still had the two bags of flour tied to its back. "He was just south of the farm, near the river. He'll be fine once we clean up that scratch from the bullet."

Helene clapped her hands with delight. "Adrien won't believe it. You must have strong *maskiki* to count such a coup, Luc."

The children arrived, caught hold of him and began dragging him toward the house, shrieking for their father to come see. Marie hung back. She was once again an intruder. She needed time to sort out her feelings for Luc and she needed that time away from the Goyette family. She needed a sanctuary.

�֎ �֎ ✖

Tom selected the two largest logs from the pile and carried them to the campfire.

"Hey, don't waste that wood, the fire is hot enough," protested a big rifleman, his mouth stuffed full of hardtack biscuit.

"Not for me it isn't." Tom threw the logs into the flames and sat beside the renewed blaze, soaking up its warmth. "It's cold already Walt,

88

and the sun has barely set. We need all the heat we can get." He tucked the ends of his greatcoat under his legs and retrieved his tin mug of tea from a flat rock at the fire's edge. He sighed as he took a sip.

Walter Grayson moved back from the fire, then turned his attention to his beloved hard-tack. He dropped a large hunk of biscuit into his tea, let it soak for a minute, then fished it out, cramming the whole thing into his mouth.

"Cheeky brat," he mumbled through his crunching teeth. "I should box your ears for you."

"You'd never catch him," a voice cried from the far side of the soldiers circled around the fire. "It would be like an elephant chasing a hornet. Ye big gormless oaf."

Alex Laidlaw always exaggerated his Scottish accent when he teased Walt. The two men were best friends, when they weren't fighting. Walter seemed to ignore the insult as he continued chewing his food.

"In fact it was a miracle those rebel buffalo hunters never managed to hit a target as big as your backside. You even look like a buffalo." Alex pushed his luck.

Walter smiled malevolently and set his cup down, carefully floating the last of his biscuit in the tea. Then he leaped suddenly to his feet and roared.

"Defend yourself, Scotchman!"

Walt was very agile despite his bulk. He launched himself into a graceful dive that carried him clear over the flames to land squarely on Laidlaw. A flurry of arms and legs lashed wildly in the ensuing wrestling match that ended a moment later with Walt sitting astride his prey.

"Get off ye big lump," Alex wheezed. "I've nae breath left in me."

"Pardon?" Walt cuffed him. "Forgotten our manners have we Scotland the *not* so brave?"

"Please remove yourself, Rifleman Grayson," he gasped. "So that I may serve you another hard-tack."

Walter beamed. "That's better, very satisfactory. I'll take some syrup on that biscuit." He stood, straightening his uniform and winked at Tom. "And get one for my friend the bugler while you're at it."

Tom smiled a thankyou. Since Paddy's death, Walter had taken over as the unofficial leader in their little group. He didn't have Paddy's wit or sense of humour but the boys in the tent all liked him and he looked after them.

"Can't get enough fighting, Grayson?" The new voice was hard, and split their circle rather than joining it. "Have to scrap with your own men?" Corporal Snell walked to the fire and helped himself to the large kettle.

"Hello, Corp. Please, have some of our tea," Grayson said sarcastically. "Got any news?"

Snell slurped and nodded. "Yup, big news. We're finally marching on Batoche. Early start tomorrow morning."

"Never!" Alex reappeared with the syrup biscuits. "You said the same thing two days ago and the week before that."

"True this time," Snell said. "Overheard the Sergeant Major and our fearless leader talking about it."

They all turned to stare at Tom. He studied his cup, pretending not to notice.

"Well Kerslake?" Alex asked. "The CSM is your uncle — is it true?"

Tom squirmed and chewed his hardtack vigorously, as though his mouth was too full to permit an answer.

"It's true then," Walt crowed. "Look how guilty the kid is! I bet he's known all day and never told us. Been holding out on his best mates. Well there's friendship for — "

"NO!" Tom interrupted before Grayson could work up an excuse to sit on him. "I mean, I don't know. I haven't seen my uncle since this morning. He spent the afternoon with Lieutenant Alderson practising skirmish drills. I did the bugle calls for Alderson, that's all. Neither of them said anything to me."

"Skirmish drills, there's a joke," Snell barked. "Supposed to be our Company Commander and he's afraid of his own shadow. Lieutenant Stutter will have us shooting each other and charging in reverse."

"Company . . . um . . . wi-wi-will . . . uh advance . . . or will we?" Alex mimicked Alderson's stumbling commands perfectly. The men laughed and repeated the words like the chorus to a song.

"He will learn. Listen!" Tom shouted them down. "He's just nervous. Give him some time."

"You've changed your tune," Snell said, studying him suspiciously. Tom shrank behind his mug, wishing his words back.

"Anyway, there is no more time." Snell addressed the circle of soldiers. "We're marching tomorrow — there'll be a fight soon." He looked back at Tom. "And our precious commander won't be ready for it."

A small convoy of three Red River carts creaked past the Caron house. They were loaded with the Goyette family's worldly possessions. One cart was pulled by a horse, the others by oxen. Adrien Goyette walked beside the first cart, using his whip to touch the oxen and keep them moving. Hélène and the children followed, leading a milk cow and two more horses. The rest of their cattle had been turned loose in the river valley. They couldn't be kept in Batoche.

Beyond Carons' the trail curved around a stand of poplars. Marie ran on ahead of the carts. The instant she passed the trees she knew she had made the right decision. The Batoche church stood tall and solid before her. In there was peace — inside those strong, white walls she would have time and solitude to think about her future. It would be her sanctuary.

The priests' house, the rectory, was just past the church. A man in a long black robe emerged from it and stared at her. Then he began walking up the trail to meet her. Marie touched her silver Mary and silently prayed for this new beginning to her life.

Adrien's carts caught up and she resumed walking beside them. Luc joined her but the loud squealing from the wooden axles prevented much conversation, for which she was thankful. She had managed to stay clear of him yesterday. They had been busy packing up the Goyette belongings to move into Batoche so there hadn't been much opportunity for Luc to be alone with her. Now if she could just find refuge with the priests.

"Is it Father Fourmond?" Adrien asked nervously. "I hope so. I can't ask Moulin for any favours. I won't give that one the satisfaction. I'd sooner . . . "

"Adrien," his wife scolded him gently. "Please. If it is *Father* Moulin, try to be civil, for my sake."

Adrien bit off his reply and snapped his whip above the lead oxen. Marie squinted at the priest. He was a short man with grey hair and a pointed white beard. He strode vigorously along the road, black skirts fluttering behind him. Her heart sank. It was Father Moulin. He was as feisty and opinionated as Monsieur Goyette — which was why they didn't get along. Gignac had been crazy to think Adrien could be in this priest's pocket. The tough little minister loved his Métis parish but he demanded obedience also.

Adrien stopped the carts and walked, scowling, to the other side, retying a rope that was already quite snug. Madame Goyette met the priest.

"Père Moulin — your blessing please."

Moulin's wrinkled face cracked a happy smile. "Madame — Hélène — how good to see you."

He made the sign of the cross and she ducked her head, repeating the sign.

"What is this?" He waved at the carts. "Where are you going?"

"To Batoche, Father. The soldiers are coming and Adrien has decided we must come in now or it will be too late."

"But not to join Riel!" Moulin's voice took a hard edge. "Not to fight?"

"*Hélas*. What choice do we have?" She wiped her brow and ran one hand nervously through her hair, tucking a loose strand back under her plaits. "The English took our wagon and flour.

They shot Adrien. It's not safe at home; we must come in."

"Of course, stay at the rectory — we will protect you." Moulin stamped his foot. "Just don't join Riel!"

Marie's heart leaped. They were in! Her prayer was answered.

"It's war, priest." Adrien moved from behind the cart to his wife's side. "I tried to stay neutral, but not after this." He touched his bandaged shoulder.

"Poof! Then go fight, foolish man — join your foolish son! Leave the children, Marie and Hélène with me."

"That is exactly what I came to ask for." Adrien spoke slowly, barely controlling his anger. "But I'll not be ordered around by the likes of you."

"Blasphemer!" Moulin shrilled. "Your family is better off with me."

"*Awas!*" Adrien banged his whip handle against the cart. "We're all going to Batoche now. I refuse to hear any more of this."

Marie felt her dream slipping away — she was going to lose her sanctuary to a stupid argument. How could she stop the bickering? She ran instinctively to Father Moulin's side. Luc reached for her but she pulled back, closer to the priest. Luc looked wildly to his mother.

The others went quiet — all eyes turned to Hélène. She put one hand on her hip, the other hand rested on her stomach. She would decide, but in her own time. A flock of sparrows chattering in the trees stopped abruptly, as though they too waited to hear her answer.

"Adrien, put away your pride for a moment. Think of the little children," Hélène finally said, stepping between the two men. "They will be much better off in the rectory if the English Army comes."

Adrien twisted the bullwhip savagely in his hands. Hélène turned to Moulin, palms outstretched. "Père, we would be happy to accept your offer for the children and Marie."

"Excellent." The priest adjusted the crucifix tucked into his waistband. "A wise choice, Madame Goyette."

"I will come with you to get them settled today," Hélène continued. "But I can't stay. If my husband must join the *notinikestamaw* then my place is beside him. He will need me to cook, make ammunition and tend his wound. I won't desert him."

She took Adrien's arm protectively.

"*Notinikestamaw!*" Moulin threw the word back at her. "You sound like those renegades from One Arrow's band. They are savages, Hélène. You're better than that!"

"My *nikawe* was one of those savages," she said tartly. "Yet she taught me compassion. She showed me what charity and love mean, Father."

"I didn't mean your mother," the priest changed his tone. "Of course not. She was a wonderful woman, but these others, with Riel . . ."

"Like my cousin?" Hélène asked. Father Moulin blushed and clasped his hands as though in prayer, finger tips under his chin. Adrien grinned broadly.

"My cousin, Sisbwepew, he is a good man. My aunt raised him to have much *kechiyimitowin* — he is not a savage." Her neck stiffened and she looked down at the short priest. "I didn't want our men to fight but between Riel and these English soldiers we are caught fast. We have no choice."

Father Moulin opened his mouth but then he hesitated. It was clearly an argument he wasn't going to win. Instead he shrugged his shoulders and smiled at the children.

"*Eh bien.* Jerome and Marguerite will be very welcome. Oh, and Marie too, of course."

Marie risked a glance at Luc. His eyes were fixed on her. For the first time she saw doubt in his expression. He was looking for a sign of loyalty from her and she felt as though she was betraying him. What could she say? Nothing, without the risk of either hurting him more or giving him false hope. She turned away and began walking to the rectory.

5
REVENGE

Who could snore the loudest? Walt and Alex seemed to be competing. Tom pulled his blankets up over his head and wriggled deeper into the mound of straw that protected him from the damp earth. It muffled the snorting racket a bit and he began to doze. Then the tent flap whipped back and one of the pickets stuck his head inside.

"Kerslake? You here?"

Tom sat up. "It can't be time already," he groaned. "It seems like these two mooses have kept me awake all night. I was just getting to sleep — "

"Stop, before I cry," the dark sentry said. "I've been on guard all night. You think I care? It's zero four-fifty of the A and M. You have to be sounding reveille in ten minutes, so shift yourself."

Tom stood, careful to keep his feet in the warm blanket while he struggled into his tunic. The jacket was stiff with frost and his breath formed damp condensation when he blew on his hands to warm them. Next came boots, like dipping his feet into cold water. Then he retrieved his bugle and stepped over the sleeping bodies to the door.

Stars were still visible overhead and in the west, but the eastern rim of the horizon was glowing. He tucked the bugle's mouthpiece under his armpit to warm it and stomped up and down to get his blood moving.

"Morning, Bugler Kerslake! Going to be a beautiful day for a hike, eh?"

Lieutenant Alderson appeared out of the half-light.

"Morning, Sir." Tom's teeth chattered and he raised one shivering hand in salute. "How are you?"

"Fine. Happy to be moving, if you must know." Alderson returned the salute briskly. "Well, I make it five o'clock: let's get to work."

"Sir, are you always so cheerful this early?" Tom asked, fitting the mouthpiece into the bugle.

"Of course!" Alderson laughed. "What could be more fun than checking pickets before dawn. Carry on, Bugler." He strolled away, whistling.

Tom took a series of deep breaths then ripped the first dozen notes of the reveille call. The loud music brought an instant howl of boos and curses from the nearby tents. Tom smiled and launched into the remainder of the tune with gusto. He felt warmer already.

G Company stood patiently at the head of the 90th Battalion, Winnipeg Rifles, waiting for the order to march. The other six companies — nearly two hundred men — were in column behind them. Following them were four cannons with their horses and limbers, then the gunners marching on foot, then a long string of supply wagons. Bringing up the rear was the Midland Battalion and some mounted scouts.

Tom's gaze swept from the distant scouts up the ranks past his own Winnipeg men and forward to the Toronto regiment at the head of the whole army — the 10th Royal Grenadiers, resplendent in crimson tunics and white belts.

Red Midlanders, blue artillerymen, green Winnipeggers and scarlet Grenadiers, all glowing like a military rainbow in the early morning sun. It was a sight that usually sent a shiver of pride down his back but this morning it somehow didn't seem right. He was nervous, and it wasn't because of the impending march into enemy territory.

The General with Boulton's Scouts were already riding down the trail. They would be watching every hill and tree for signs of a rebel ambush. A long shriek from the *Northcote*'s whistle echoed up from the river valley and several horses whinnied in reply. The huge paddlewheel began turning, churning white foam out from the boat's stern as she gathered way and moved out into the river. They would meet her at Gabriel's Crossing, twenty kilometres downstream, this afternoon.

Finally the command was relayed down the line and the men shouldered their rifles. The long column of soldiers, horses, wagons, and guns began to march.

"AT LAST!" Snell's voice boomed out. "We're shaking the dust of Fish Creek from our boots, boys, never to return." He was rewarded with a loud cheer from G Company.

Never to return — the thought repeated in Tom's mind. Then a sudden surge of panic overpowered him. He looked desperately toward the crosses on a small rise a few metres away. It was such a tiny, pathetic patch of lonely ground surrounded by miles of prairie and bush. There was Paddy's cross — the last one.

"Bide here with me Tommy." The cross seemed to quote Paddy's last words. They couldn't just leave him here in this wilderness and never return. He bolted from the ranks and ran to the grave.

"Hey! Back into ranks, Kerslake!" The Corporal's command chased him but Tom ignored it. He had to see Paddy — say something — do something. He touched the cross; his thoughts were a wild jumble inside his head.

A hand fell on his shoulder and Tom looked up. Lieutenant Alderson smiled at him. "What is it?"

"Can't go!" Tom blurted out. "Can't just leave Paddy." Tears leaked from his eyes and ran down his cheeks. He waved his arm at the broad river valley. "NOT here, all alone out in this God forsaken . . . "

A sob came from his stomach and hit his throat, cutting off his voice. Then he started crying hard. He'd never cried for Paddy before, not even at the funeral, and now he couldn't imagine ever stopping. He turned away from the marching soldiers and wept. Alderson's arm went round his shoulders and held tight.

"Tom, did you know that my father has a lot of money?"

Tom shook his head angrily. Who cared about Alderson's money?

"Well, we're actually rich," he continued. "And I promise you, on my life, that we'll not leave Paddy here."

Tom sucked in a shaky breath. "What? How?"

When we get back to Winnipeg I will hire some men and return to Fish Creek. We'll pick up Paddy and all the other Winnipeg boys lying here. We'll put them on the train and bring them home to be buried properly, in Winnipeg."

Tom blinked his eyes clear of tears. "Can you do that?"

Alderson laughed. "Just watch me. I promise you it will be done."

Tom felt the panic and fear ebb gradually away. "You have family in Winnipeg. Father and sister I understand?" Alderson squeezed his shoulder. "Did they know Flaherty?" Tom shook his head. "That's it, then. You can take your family to visit Paddy. Tell them all about him, what he was like."

A sudden vision of Violet with flowers at Paddy's grave struck Tom. She and Paddy were nearly the same age. They could have been friends. Could still be friends in a way — if he did as Alderson suggested.

A robin sang its mating song from the trees near the river. He breathed easily now and the tears stopped.

"Let's go, Bugler Kerslake." Alderson plucked at Tom's sleeve. "At the double."

Adrien Goyette looked down at Marie, considering her request. She was much too thin. He wondered if she was getting enough to eat.

"Will you do it?" she prompted. "Please?"

And very determined, he thought. The "please" was not given easily. Her black eyes squinted up at him, demanding an answer.

"It's Gareau's job — he's being paid to build the church — ask him to do it," he snapped irritably. "Besides, I've been up all night watching the English camp. I'm too tired right now."

He touched his heels to the horse's flanks and it began to plod forward. Small mushroom-shaped clouds of dust popped up as each hoof clopped onto the packed dirt.

"Monsieur Gareau won't come back to Batoche until the soldiers have gone." Marie spoke quickly, jogging by his side trying to hold him with her words. "He thinks they will smash it with cannonballs anyway, so what's the point in finishing?"

She grabbed the corner of the bit and pulled the horse's head back. It stopped walking and cast a large brown eye on her. "But Père Caribou says that if the soldiers see a cross they won't shoot because they'll know it's a church."

She hefted the heavy wooden crucifix up, resting the butt on her hip, and stared hard into his eyes. "So for us to be safe . . . you have to nail the cross onto the top of the church." She stopped short of mentioning his children. She couldn't deliberately embarrass him.

There was a long silence. Goyette returned her stare, pushing it back, but she refused to look away. A meadowlark's bubbling song broke the trance and his resolve. He slid down from the saddle and passed her the lines.

"A deal," he smiled weakly. "You water my horse then go back to the rectory — get Father Moulin to make me some tea." He lifted the cross easily with one hand. "And I'll hang your precious cross, Marie. After all, as you so tactfully did not say, my children are sheltering in the church too."

"*Merci*, Monsieur Goyette. I'll bring your tea out myself and — "

"No!" Adrien stopped her. "It was Father Moulin who sent you to ambush me — it's his crucifix. I want him to bring my drink."

Marie hesitated, trying to pick the right words. "It was my idea to ask you, not Père Caribou's." Then she added with a touch of defiance, "It's his church, but it's my cross."

He set the cross on the ground. "Oh, so it's just a coincidence that last night when I passed through on my way to Tourond's, Moulin ordered me to raise the cross?"

He turned his head and spat over his shoulder. "I told him what to do with his orders. And now this morning you have the exact same notion?"

"Well, almost." She led his horse back down the trail toward the well before he could change his mind. "Père Caribou said you were busy last night. He said you would do it this morning if I asked you — but it *is* my Cross — it was my idea, originally."

Goyette laughed. "Père says this, Père says that," he mimicked. "You're very sure of yourself, eh? You better not let Father Moulin hear you call him Père Caribou. Just make sure he gets my tea; it will teach him some priestly humility."

"Thank you, Papa!" She ran down the ravine toward the well at the bottom. How easily she called him Papa and how unfair that her real father was a man whose only virtues were his long absences.

The horse nuzzled her shoulder as she worked the pump. Its soft nose pushed impatiently and knocked a strand of black hair loose from the single plait that hung down her back. She stopped pumping, tucked the hair behind her ear and shoved him away. A moment later he returned, puffing moist air over her neck. She gave him the water.

The sun cleared the rim of the coulee and shot a single bright ray onto the side of her face. She turned, seeking the warmth. It was May, yet there was still a heavy frost on the grass — that seemed unfair too. It should be green and warm, not cold, leafless and brown. Winter instead of spring; soldiers coming to make war; and, a substitute for a father. It was unfair.

At least living with the nuns she had some freedom from her worries about Luc. And her cross, that was good too. She shaded her eyes and looked up. The church stood above the skyline. Sunlight on church whitewash — pure, clean, even sparkling.

Adrien, cross in one hand, hammer dangling from his belt, climbed up the ladder which lay flat on the roof's slope. Yes, it was needed for their protection. If he hadn't done it, she would have. It was her crucifix and it would make this her home.

"What! Me? Personally wait on him?" Father Moulin's stern little face wrinkled with outrage. "That man's great sin is pride. Pride and stubborn conceit."

"Oh, Father, it's not such a big thing. I've already made the tea." Marie held a pitcher out for him. "And besides, that's exactly what he says about you. He said: 'Father Moulin is too proud for a priest — he needs to be more humble.'"

"I'll show him Humble!" The angry priest snatched the jug from her and strode out of the kitchen. "I've got more humility in my little finger than he does in his whole . . . "

The door slammed. Moulin passed in front of the kitchen window and crossed the open space between the rectory and the church. Adrien was hammering the last nails into the base of the cross. It looked ridiculously small, perched atop the tall roof, but that didn't matter. It filled Marie with a sense of contentment. She touched the silver Mary again. Mary's son's cross was up now, on high where it belonged.

She began to cut bread for the Goyette children. Jerome and Marguerite waited in uncharacteristic silence for their breakfast.

111

"Oh, Marie. I thought Père Caribou was going to explode when you told him what Papa said." Jerome's eyes were round with disbelief. "I'm too scared of Père to even talk to him sometimes."

"Don't worry, he really likes your father. They just argue. Now eat up and when you're finished you can go see Papa — maybe he'll share his tea with you."

She left the two children chattering over their food and climbed the stairs to the second floor gable window. The open yard in front of the rectory dropped down into the water-well ravine. Beyond that, about a half kilometre distant, a cemetery lay on the crown of the Saskatchewan River bank. Thick woods lined both sides of the cemetery and filled the ravine up to the well. Dozens of men scurried in and out of the treeline, wielding axes, mattocks and shovels — digging rifle pits.

When the Canadian Army arrived, the Métis would be ready. "A warm reception" were the words Papa — Monsieur Goyette — had used. The freshly-scarred earth looked more like a row of open graves and the thought made her shiver. Why did they have to fight? What would it prove? The Cree from One Arrow's band said the bend in the Saskatchewan was *aski* for the Métis because the Métis got their life from it. Even Père agreed. He said God gave it to the Métis people for their *kikinaw* and there was an end of it. But no, Riel had to stir up trouble over something they already owned; first with the priests, then the police, and now the whole Canadian Army was coming to shoot and burn and . . .

Familiar tears stung her; she wiped them on her sleeve. No more weeping for them. Adrien and Luc and all the others had made their choice — they didn't have to join Dumont and his rebels. Yet Adrien still attended mass. How could he fight for Riel on the one hand and pray in the church as well? There was no reason or sense to it and no point in her trying to understand.

She returned to the kitchen. She would haul more water from the well: the children could help her. Then they would take it out to the men digging pits when Père Caribou wasn't watching. She couldn't join their fight but at least she could take them something to drink.

Were her own loyalties as confusing as Luc and Adrien's after all?

"When did they march?" Gabriel demanded.

"A little after seven this morning — two hours ago." There were nearly a hundred Métis men surrounding him, waiting on Adrien's every word. "They are on the river trail — heading for your place, Gabriel. They have a steamer with them but I doubt they'll go farther than your ferry today."

Dumont stood silent for a moment then raised his voice so all could hear.

"We can expect the English tomorrow, *Mes Amis!*" He slapped *Le Petit*'s stock. "And we are ready for them! *On les mouchera!*"

The crowd murmured at this news. Luc felt the tension but it was controlled. Gabriel was right; they had dug in very cleverly. The soldiers would have a hard fight breaking into Batoche. The hills overlooking the village were ringed with pits.

"Spend this evening with your families," Dumont continued. "I want every man and his provisions in his pit by midnight. We will not be caught napping."

"Everyone here, Corporal?" Jim Kerslake asked.

"All present, Sarn't Major." Snell nodded to the four men lined up behind him. Each man carried an axe.

"Well, let's get it over with then," Alderson ordered. "Carry on, Corporal."

Snell and the axemen marched off in single file down the path leading to Gabriel's ferry crossing. The lieutenant and Jim followed.

"Sir!" Tom's shout stopped them. "Can I come with you?"

The two men turned and waited for him to catch up.

"No need for you to come, Tom," his uncle frowned.

"Quite so," Alderson looked slightly embarrassed. "A nasty job: you shouldn't be involved."

"Nasty job?" Tom was puzzled. "I thought you were going to burn Dumont out?"

"We are," Alderson said. "But burning a man's home is a dirty job. We're soldiers — not arsonists."

Tom stood firm, hoping silence would be better than arguing. Alderson slapped his leg impatiently.

"Very well then," he capitulated. They continued down the trail toward the crossing. The lieutenant barely touched the ground with his right foot and winced when he did put any weight on it.

"How's the foot, sir?" Jim asked.

"One huge blister, from heel to toe," Alderson grimaced. "I'll be fine by tomorrow."

"New boots," Tom piped up, glad to change the subject from house burning. "The first twenty miles out of Fort Qu'Appelle my boots nearly killed me. You should drain the blisters and bandage your feet."

Alderson shot him a pained look. G Company had marched over two hundred miles through spring mud to reach Fish Creek. They were hardened veterans. Today's trip of thirteen miles had been a stroll for them, but agony for a tenderfoot like him.

Most of Dumont's stable had been torn down already and the wood used to build barricades on the *Northcote*'s decks. Only the store and house were left standing. A party of Grenadiers were manhandling a billiard table through the narrow store doorway.

"I don't believe it — how did Dumont get a pool table all the way out here?" Jim exclaimed. "It's a beauty too, look at the cloth."

The grenadiers struggled down to the river shore and hauled the table up the gangplank onto the steamboat.

"The steamer crew are going to war in style."

Tom laughed, but Alderson scowled.

"Why would he risk all this?" he said to no one in particular.

"Who, sir?" Tom asked.

"Gabriel Dumont," Alderson answered. "A fine house, a decent farm, a ferry business, even a pool table and a washing machine." The lieutenant shook his head. "Why risk losing all this to start a rebellion? These men aren't savages; what could have driven them to fight?"

The small group fell silent. Anger grew inside Tom like an incoming tide. Why was his own officer siding with the enemy?

"Well it's too late to turn back now," Uncle Jim said. "For whatever reason they *did* start a rebellion. It's our job to put it down, not understand it."

"Of course, Sergeant Major," Alderson replied curtly. "Carry on Corporal, fire the buildings."

"Yes SIR!" Snell whooped. "Let's build a bonfire." He almost skipped with delight as he led the men to the small store. Tom went with them. Two soldiers climbed onto the roof and began chopping a hole in it. The others entered the store, smashed the one small window and began cutting up the furniture. They piled the splinters in one corner and stuffed straw at the bottom of the wood.

"Alright boys — here she goes!" Snell called to the men on the roof. He knelt and struck a match. It flared brightly as Snell touched it to the straw. In seconds the kindling was blazing. Several long flames licked at the log walls until one caught and held like a yellow and blue ribbon. Then another and another. Smoke roiled off the pile and whipped swiftly upward through the hole in the roof.

Tom felt the heat; it was warm and comforting. Smoke stung his eyes to tears and burned his nose, but he just sniffed. The strong scent of a burning rebel home seemed proof that the Rifles could hit back and hurt their enemy. He wanted the feel and the smell of this fire. It fanned an anger inside him. Then the flames seemed to jump up to the ceiling and Snell was pulling him back out the door. He emerged into the fresh air but turned back immediately to stand as close as he could manage to the store.

Flames began to shoot through the window and roof. Heat billowed from the open door, pushing him away, scorching the skin on his forehead and cheeks.

"Bloody shame, I still say, Sarn't Major." It was Alderson's voice, from behind him. "Rebel or not, it's an awful sight when a man's home is destroyed."

Tom's rage soared with the fire. He could scarcely hold it back; it shot up inside like the flames. He wanted to scream at his uncle and the officer. Dumont might be the one who shot Paddy. What's a burned house — what is it compared to somebody's life? Did they care more for a rebel store than their own men?

Alderson's eyes hardened, his jaw clenched, "Its a mean kind of vengeance to take, no mistake about it."

"Aye, sir." Jim nodded in agreement.

Tom turned sharply, driven by a wild urge to let the scream go, whatever the consequences. His uncle calmly stroking his moustache. The young boy-officer mewing like a kitten over a burned shack. Pathetic, weak, no feeling for Paddy lying cold and dead.

For one long, awful moment Tom's fury was mixed with a rush of grief for Paddy and he nearly cried. But he held on, forcing it back and pushing it down. In its place a coldness crept in. His anger turned from sudden flame to hard ice.

Vengeance, Alderson's word. Of course! Tom remembered Snell. Revenge was what they were taking — legitimate revenge. No need for anger with this unblooded young officer. He just didn't understand; Paddy wasn't a real person to the Lieutenant.

Jim was shocked. He'd rarely seen a face like this on a grown man — never on a boy. Tom's eyes were fixed with an ugly, brutish stare. His jaw and mouth were set in an animal ferocity that was grotesque.

"Tom?" he asked. "What's wrong? Are you ill? Step clear of the fire."

His nephew marched woodenly to them, then looked back at the fire.

"Tom," Jim repeated. "What is it?"

Tom half turned. "Nothing sir." His voice was hoarse. "A little smoke maybe. Permission to carry on, Lieutenant Alderson?"

Alderson exchanged a worried glance with the CSM then nodded. Tom ran toward Gabriel Dumont's house where Snell and the others were chopping the doors off their hinges.

"Tom!" His uncle's voice, not the Sergeant Major's bark, called to him. He stopped but did not turn around. Jim walked to his side.

"I should have finished our talk at Paddy's grave. I've left this too long," he said apologetically. "I wasn't sure you would understand."

"Understand what, sir," Tom answered calmly.

"That Paddy was a soldier and soldiers get killed in war." Jim pulled his shoulder, forcing him to stand face to face. "We grow to hate our enemies Tom, it's natural. But we can never even the score — it's not a checkers game. Paddy's gone and more will follow him. That's how it works. We'll only stop it by defeating the rebels. That's why we burn Dumont out. To crush the rebellion, not for revenge."

Tom heard the words and knew his uncle was probably right. But the cold inside him wouldn't let him accept it. He gritted his teeth and avoided Jim's stare.

"Don't grow to like it, Tommy," Jim urged. "Don't let it get you or you'll end up like Snell.

Remember how you were raised. Don't turn into something your father or Violet would be ashamed of."

Like Snell? Shame stabbed him. Snell was a hard case — vicious. It was probably no coincidence that Walt and Alex had refused to volunteer for the burning job. In truth, Paddy wouldn't have asked for it either. This was just a home, not much different from his home. So what was he doing here?

He was looking for answers. Thoughts of Vi and father and home gave him a little comfort. Smoke was beginning to trickle out of the upper windows of Dumont's house. Tom felt the hatred begin to melt. And yet he was unable to stifle a sensation of fierce glee. Why not burn Dumont's house for revenge? Revenge felt good.

6
A Vision

The Canadians didn't come. The scouts said the army had turned away from the river and was camped inland a few miles southeast of the church. They would come tomorrow for certain. Luc swung his mattock hard at the thought. The pits could be deeper — better protection from artillery fire if you were in a deep pit. This one would give them a perfect view of the Englishmen if they used the trail past the Rectory, while the screen of poplar trees directly in front of the trench would make it invisible.

Luc slammed the big pick down again, loosening a hunk of earth. The freshly-turned soil smelled of spring: a moist odour of ground recently thawed and come back to life. It was May — the high acres north of their pasture would be dry enough to seed. He and Father should be ploughing that land right now. What *would* they do for a crop this year? Would the soldiers burn the farm? Maybe it was destroyed already. He unleashed a flurry of mattock strokes then stepped back while Moise and Eleazar shovelled the loose dirt out.

He sat on the edge of the trench and peered through the bushes toward the rectory. For the past two days Marie and the children had made tea for the men but there was no sign of her this morning. Maybe he would go see her when they'd finished digging. Every day she seemed more settled with the Priests and every day she seemed to drift farther away from him. He had to see her, even for a few minutes, just to stay connected. If he didn't then she might break from him for ever.

"He's at it again!" Moise cackled.

"Dreaming of HER," Eleazar winked. "These young roosters are all the same, Moise. He's *saketawah kosiwin*. Good thing we're here to do all the work."

Luc retrieved his mattock and swung it rapidly, producing a series of deep gouges in the floor of the pit. "You two ancients wouldn't even have scratched the surface without me. The English army would catch you hiding like *deux vieux lapins* in the grass."

Moise and Eleazar were old men — old enough to be his grandfathers — but they were hard, lean old men.

"HA! You dig like a badger little Goyette but you'll be happy to have two old rabbits beside you when the soldiers come."

"I'd rather be with my father," Luc said more seriously. "Gabriel said he didn't want us together. I don't think he trusts us."

Moise and Eleazar glanced at each other and began shovelling out the pit.

"He's wrong though. I've proved myself, and father volunteered to fight. Dumont should know he can depend on us."

Luc thumped the mattock a few more times. "Eleazar, what have you heard? Is Gabriel still against the Goyettes?"

"Oh, Dumont has great faith in you," Eleazar shrugged. "He wants you separated from your father for your own good. If the soldiers attack here, or if one of their cannonballs hit this trench, then both men from one family are gone. If you are split, then maybe one survives."

Luc put his mattock aside. He was surprised by the notion. "You think it will get that bad?"

Moise nodded. "Bad enough. We are only a few hundred — counting the Dakota and Cree. If the Canadians are determined . . . well, we can't hold here forever."

He laughed at Luc's sober face. "Cheer up! Eleazar and me, we fought the Sioux down south. Remember Eleazar! They surprised four of our men out cutting wood in the Cypress Hills. It took two hundred Oglala Sioux warriors to kill four woodcutters. But then thirty Métis men gave chase — well, twenty-nine men and Eleazar here."

Eleazar swatted his old friend. "Thirty men," he took up the story. "We caught the Sioux and made them pay, I'll tell you." A fierce grin creased his leathery old face. "Then four years later those Oglala wiped out Custer."

Moise fixed Luc with a hard stare. "We'll make these Englishmen dance a pretty jig, never fear."

Luc forced a quick smile and resumed his work. Now, for certain, he would have to talk to Marie.

Marie could not bring herself to speak. How could she know? Was it so obvious?

"You must tell him, Marie. It's not fair to let him think he has a claim on you."

"Ah . . . yes, Madame. I promise to speak to him. It is the only fair thing to do."

Hélène kissed her on the brow. "You know, we think of you as our daughter. If you need me, come to the village any time." Marie followed her to the rectory door. The children each seized one of their mother's hands and they set off to the Dakota camp.

Luc's mother had made the trip up from the village on the eve of the battle to ask for fair treatment for her son. Marie couldn't back away from such a request. She climbed the stairs to the second floor. A tiny door in one wall opened onto a narrow passageway containing a ladder that led up to the attic. She climbed up and sat heavily on the floor, her elbows resting on the ledge of a small window. It was a quiet, almost secret place. The others rarely ventured up here. She used it to be on her own, as a place to think.

Far below, men were digging pits at the edge of the trees near the cemetery. Luc was in there somewhere. His mother was right, of course. And

Madame Goyette shook her finger at Marguerite and Jerome. "Are you minding Marie? I hope you have been good."

The two little children nodded their heads. "*Oui, maman*," they sang.

"Have you seen the Sioux warriors, *maman*?" Jerome asked, balancing on one foot, with his arms outstretched. "They are big and they have different feathers from us."

"Yes and their ponies run so fast they fly." Marguerite whipped one hand past her mother. "They paint their ponies too, but Marie won't let us go to their camp. Can we go?"

Hélène smiled. "The Dakota are different from us. Marie was right, you can't go there alone. But if you are polite then I will take you for a visit before I return to the village."

This caused squeals of delight.

"Now go outside and play. I have to talk to Marie."

"Hop race! Hop race!" Jerome announced, and a moment later they were bounding for the door as racing jack rabbits.

"Thank you, Marie," she said, closing the door behind the hoppers. "It is so much easier for me in the village knowing you are caring for those two little squirrels here at the rectory. I know you will keep them safe."

She paused, thinking like her husband how thin and pale Marie had become. "Come, sit with me." Hélène took Marie by the hand and led her to the visitors' bench beside the stove. She put one arm around Marie's shoulders.

"Sister Alphonsine tells me you work too hard, helping her with the kitchen, tending the children, and constantly serving the priests. Why don't you slow down a bit?"

"I'm fine, Madame," Marie reassured her. "Jerome and Marguerite are like my brother and sister, they're no trouble. And I'm happy here. I love the church. Alphonsine teaches me many things — it just feels like I'm meant to be here."

Hélène softly brushed the back of her hand against Marie's cheek. "Do you know this song?"

My fate is O so hard since I am forced to still
My heart's love deeply hidden in a convent
'gainst my will.

Marie began to rock gently back and forth and joined in singing:

I'll break, I think, my chain
To see my lover dear.
He is a smart young Captain
And my heart desires him here."

They laughed and hugged at the end of the verse.

"Adrien and I sang that old song to each other many, many times when we travelled on the buffalo hunts." Hélène looked into Marie's eyes. "Are you truly happy here, *hidden in a convent?*"

Marie rose and walked to the east window. The church stood directly opposite the window and her gaze was drawn to the cross at the roof's peak. Her cross. The thought gave her a warm sense of contentment. She touched her silver Mary.

"Yes, I truly am." She turned to face Hélène. "Besides, the women at the village suspect me because my father sides with the English. I'm better to keep busy up here with the priests."

"I understand." Madame Goyette nodded. "What about Luc — your *smart young captain?*"

Marie's heart beat faster. "Yes, Madame?"

"You know how he feels about you. But I think you don't have the same feelings for him. Am I right?"

now that she had promised, there really was no way out. Yet she recoiled from the idea of rejecting him totally. Why? Because maybe she did love him — maybe she shouldn't turn away from him.

A small framed print hung above the window. It was a picture of the Virgin Mary with a gold halo painted over her head. The gold glowed in the dim attic light. Marie took it down and the Virgin's eyes seemed to move, following her.

Marie knelt and held the painting before her. "What should I do? What can I say to him?" she asked, but Mary would not answer.

Perhaps she was asking the wrong question.

"Is this my home? Am I meant for the church?"

The gold halo sparkled for an instant — Marie blinked. Was that a yes? It must be. The church *was* her home. Or was it? Hélène's song came back to her and with it the thought that perhaps Luc was her heart's love. The same old confusions — the same old doubts. Except she couldn't afford them any longer; there was no more time. She would see Luc tonight before the enemy arrived.

�֎ �֎ ✶

Hélène Goyette realized there might be a problem as soon as they drew near the Dakota camp. There were only a couple of lodges and they were in a sad state. Some of the skins were worn through and others were patched with pieces of canvas, even cotton. There was no order to the cooking fires; in fact there was no evidence of an organized camp at all. This meant that there were no women here. It was a shelter for a war party, nothing more. She had planned to introduce herself to the women according to proper manners and ask permission to see the ponies. But no women . . . she hesitated.

A half dozen Dakota men sat outside the largest tent with their backs to her. She did not want to intrude and wasn't sure how to get their attention. A horse and rider approached, branching off the St. Laurent trail that ran past the east end of the camp. A second man walked beside the horse. Both were armed, but both were Cree. Probably coming from One Arrow's Reserve. Here was an opportunity — she waved to them. The rider waved back and veered toward her.

Then he waved again and kicked the horse into a trot. What luck! It was her cousin

Sisbwepew. The other man she recognized as Meitatinas, but she didn't know him very well. Father Moulin's words suddenly came back to her, "renegade savages", and she laughed to herself. Sisebwepew was stubborn, a renegade even, but certainly not a savage. His French was better than hers and he could converse with Dakota, Blackfoot and Englishman alike. He slid easily from the horse and gaped with mock astonishment at the two children.

"*Awas!* We are saved! The Goyette warriors have arrived. Surely now the police will run in fear."

He was a big man with a voice deep as thunder. The musket nestled neatly in the crook of a muscular arm and his beaded leggings gave him a warlike air. The children slunk shyly behind their Mother's skirts.

"Hélène," he smiled. I saw Adrien at the pits yesterday. Never thought he would join Riel."

"We had no option," Hélène replied. "He was shot."

"Yes, I saw the wound." He touched her arm. "I thought of you then. Two of your men fighting. Luc nearly gone at Tourond's Coulee. It must have been difficult."

"Thank you, Sisebwepew." Hélène opened her palms to him. "How are your mother and your wife?"

"In very fine health. They find fault with me though. A man can stand an old woman scolding or a young one — but not both." He winked at Marguerite. "That's why I had to leave and come fight for Riel. The police bullets are kinder to Sisebwepew than his own women!"

"We're not Métis soldiers," Marguerite replied seriously. "But we would like to see the Sioux ponies; they run faster than an eagle flies."

Hélène squeezed her hand.

"Um, we would like to see the ponies PLEASE, *monsieur*."

"Then you will see them, come on."

He led them past the Dakota men. "We are going to look at your fine horses," he called. "The children think Sioux *sunka wankan kinyan*."

"Horses that fly?" one of the Sioux asked, waving his arms like wings. "Compared to your Cree cart horses — they *do* fly!" The other Dakota laughed.

Sisebwepew and Meitatinas returned the laughter but it seemed forced to Hélène. Most of the Métis men had lost their horses to English rifle fire during the fight at Tourond's Coulee.

"What do you make of the Sioux?" she asked quietly.

He frowned. "We fought them and the Blackfoot when I was young. Your people fought them very hard in Montana several times. The Sioux are our enemy I suppose. But this Canadian Army, they are an enemy to everyone. If we lose now, then Métis, Cree, Sioux — all of us — lose forever. So I am happy to have Dakota on my side."

"You trust them then?" Hélène asked. "We heard they left Tourond's battle early."

Sisebwepew stopped walking and faced her. There was anger in his face but he kept it from his voice. "How many men died for Riel at Tourond's, Hélène, do you know?"

She thought for a moment then answered carefully. "Yes, Four. Old Vermette, Pierre Parenteau, . . . "

"No, Hélène," he rumbled. "That is what Riel says — four. There were six. The other two were Dakota Sioux. Left behind by the Métis."

Hélène blushed and lowered her eyes. "I did not know."

Sisebwepew resumed walking. He nudged her and smiled, "Now you do."

They neared the poplar bluff where the ponies were gathered. Marguerite and Jerome ran ahead. "Ho!" Sisebwepew shouted. "Be careful of their wings."

Eleazar looped the twine deftly around the log and the stake that supported it. Luc heaved the log up into place and held it while Eleazar snugged it down and tied off the twine. Their pit was over a metre deep and two metres long. Earth was piled high in front of the trench and two stout logs were tied together on top of the earth. Smaller sticks were wedged between the logs so that there was an open slit between them.

Luc jumped into the pit. Crouching slightly he obtained a clear view through the slit. He could shoot from here and be almost completely protected. Moise was placing twigs and leaves over the freshly-dug earth. From a distance their trench was invisible. To his left and right were more trenches situated so that no one could pass through without coming under a Métis gun.

Tonight women from the village would bring up food and ammunition. Then tomorrow . . . He couldn't wait till tomorrow. It might be too late once the fighting started. He climbed out of the pit and set off for the Rectory.

The late afternoon sun hung over the church, just above her cross. Marie stood beyond the church while the children ran to hide. She was supposed to count to one hundred, then go find them, but she lost track of her numbers and her mind wandered again to Luc. How to tell him about her feelings?

The cross cast a long shadow — it reached across the grass toward her. "The truth" it seemed to say, pointing the way. Just tell him the truth. She could not love him, not yet. She needed time to decide — simple and clear. She turned and began walking toward the trenches near the cemetery, resolved to confront her dilemma.

"Hey Marie!" A little voice squealed indignantly from behind the woodpile. They *always* hid behind the woodpile. "Why aren't you hunting for us? Where are you going?"

Marie kept walking and yelled back over her shoulder, "I can't play anymore. You two stay at the rectory; I'll be back in a minute."

"Aw, you promised to play with us." The whiny voices faded as Marie sped up. She had to keep going before she lost her nerve.

Luc descended the ravine to the well at the bottom. He dropped his hat on the grass, rolled up his sleeves and pumped rapidly on the handle. Water gushed out the spout and he sluiced it over his hands then splashed it on his face and scrubbed away the dirt. His shirt-tail served as a towel. He was just retrieving his hat when a figure appeared at the top of the ravine. Marie stood facing the setting sun and waved to him. She seemed to shine in the heavy yellow light.

Marie walked down the ravine and stopped opposite him. She did not speak but her eyes held him steadily. The familiar sensation hit him — like she was a part of him. He was unwilling to make a noise lest he break the spell that had settled on them. Instead he studied her long black hair, plaited down her back, and re-memorized how her cheeks and mouth formed such a kind, beautiful face.

"They will be here tomorrow, the Canadians," she said at last. "So I have to speak to you, now. In a day's time who knows what will become of us."

He nodded mutely, dreading that this might be the end and he would be helpless to prevent it.

"My father and mother serve the Canadians. I have no brother or sister, so I have no family of my own." Her eyes lost their confidence and flickered away from him. She began talking rapidly, gushing like the pump.

"I have come to think of you — the Goyettes — as my family. You are my brother, Luc, and I would do anything for you. I would risk anything for you, because I love you . . . " She stopped, as though surprised by her own words. His heart thumped with anticipation.

"I love you as my brother," she said firmly. "But you don't love me as a sister, do you?"

He stood rigid as her question hit him. Pride flared for a moment, trying to pretend she hadn't hurt him.

"You think we will be together in that church one day, married?"

He found his voice. "Yes Marie, I do. And I won't give you up. We are more than brother and sister. I can feel it, even if you can't."

"There is another family for me, Luc. It has a stronger bond. God is calling to me. I don't know what for yet — I'm confused. Sometimes I think he wants me for himself . . . "

"*Une Soeur?*" Luc burst out. "You'd leave me to be a nun!"

She found herself smiling, calm now that it was in the open. Take vows as a nun — it was a possibility she had scarcely dared to consider. Is that what Mary's picture was trying to tell her?

"Maybe, and maybe not. I'm not certain. That's what I've come to tell you, Luc. Sometimes I also think He wants me to go to you. The truth is that I really don't know what will happen. So for now we are brother and sister."

She took his hands, still damp from the well water. She kissed each one softly and squeezed them tight. Then she turned and ran up the hill. Luc stayed for a long time. The sunlight crept out of the ravine and shadows followed it in. His hands were warm, and tingled from her kiss.

Anger, pride and fear were all gone. They had left with Marie. He felt a strange contentment. It might be right between them yet, but he couldn't chase her. She would have to come to him.

⚒ ⚒ ⚒

"Sleep on your rifles tonight, boys." The Sergeant Major's voice boomed across the company tent lines. "Cartridge boxes for your pillows!"

Half the men in Tom's tent were out on picket duty — the guard had been doubled.

"Alderson says we're only six miles from Batoche," Walt said. "And the rebels still haven't raided us yet . . . " His voice trailed off.

Alex and Tom were already rolled up in their blankets but they wore all their clothes. Tom's bugle was tucked in near his belly. Alex's big Snider Enfield lay next to his arm.

"Which means tonight is their last chance to hit us before we reach Batoche," Alex snapped. "We know that already, Walt. Quit grumbling and get some kip — our watch is midnight to reveille."

"Can't sleep, lying on this rifle." Walt thrashed around trying to make himself comfortable.

"Don't forget to call me early, Walt," Tom yawned. "I have to blow reveille at four sharp."

The last of the sunset glowed on the west side of their tent. Tom wondered what the rebels were doing tonight. Were they frightened? He hoped so. The Winnipeg Rifles — no, the Little Black Devils — were ready to send them all to the devil. The day of reckoning was here.

A loud snort interrupted his thoughts.

"Can't sleep?" Alex muttered. "Yon great oaf was snoring like a pig before his head was down. Give him a kick will you Tommy?"

Tom pulled his arm free and shoved Walt's head to one side. The snoring ceased abruptly. Wriggling back down into his blanket Tom closed his eyes. *The rebels will pay, Paddy. We will make them pay tomorrow.*

A lantern shed just enough light for Luc to see half their pit. His mother sat beside him while Moise and Eleazar crouched opposite them. She had brought *galettes*, smoked beef, and *taureau* in a linen bag that was wrapped in oilcloth. There were also forty shells for Luc's shotgun. She had

Madame Goyette shook her finger at Marguerite and Jerome. "Are you minding Marie? I hope you have been good."

The two little children nodded their heads. "*Oui, maman*," they sang.

"Have you seen the Sioux warriors, *maman*?" Jerome asked, balancing on one foot, with his arms outstretched. "They are big and they have different feathers from us."

"Yes and their ponies run so fast they fly." Marguerite whipped one hand past her mother. "They paint their ponies too, but Marie won't let us go to their camp. Can we go?"

Hélène smiled. "The Dakota are different from us. Marie was right, you can't go there alone. But if you are polite then I will take you for a visit before I return to the village."

This caused squeals of delight.

"Now go outside and play. I have to talk to Marie."

"Hop race! Hop race!" Jerome announced, and a moment later they were bounding for the door as racing jack rabbits.

"Thank you, Marie," she said, closing the door behind the hoppers. "It is so much easier for me in the village knowing you are caring for those two little squirrels here at the rectory. I know you will keep them safe."

She paused, thinking like her husband how thin and pale Marie had become. "Come, sit with me." Hélène took Marie by the hand and led her to the visitors' bench beside the stove. She put one arm around Marie's shoulders.

"Sister Alphonsine tells me you work too hard, helping her with the kitchen, tending the children, and constantly serving the priests. Why don't you slow down a bit?"

"I'm fine, Madame," Marie reassured her. "Jerome and Marguerite are like my brother and sister, they're no trouble. And I'm happy here. I love the church. Alphonsine teaches me many things — it just feels like I'm meant to be here."

Hélène softly brushed the back of her hand against Marie's cheek. "Do you know this song?"

*My fate is O so hard since I am forced to still
My heart's love deeply hidden in a convent
'gainst my will.*

Marie began to rock gently back and forth and joined in singing:

I'll break, I think, my chain
To see my lover dear.
He is a smart young Captain
And my heart desires him here."

They laughed and hugged at the end of the verse.

"Adrien and I sang that old song to each other many, many times when we travelled on the buffalo hunts." Hélène looked into Marie's eyes. "Are you truly happy here, *hidden in a convent?*"

Marie rose and walked to the east window. The church stood directly opposite the window and her gaze was drawn to the cross at the roof's peak. Her cross. The thought gave her a warm sense of contentment. She touched her silver Mary.

"Yes, I truly am." She turned to face Hélène. "Besides, the women at the village suspect me because my father sides with the English. I'm better to keep busy up here with the priests."

"I understand." Madame Goyette nodded. "What about Luc — your *smart young captain?*"

Marie's heart beat faster. "Yes, Madame?"

"You know how he feels about you. But I think you don't have the same feelings for him. Am I right?"

Marie could not bring herself to speak. How could she know? Was it so obvious?

"You must tell him, Marie. It's not fair to let him think he has a claim on you."

"Ah . . . yes, Madame. I promise to speak to him. It is the only fair thing to do."

Hélène kissed her on the brow. "You know, we think of you as our daughter. If you need me, come to the village any time." Marie followed her to the rectory door. The children each seized one of their mother's hands and they set off to the Dakota camp.

Luc's mother had made the trip up from the village on the eve of the battle to ask for fair treatment for her son. Marie couldn't back away from such a request. She climbed the stairs to the second floor. A tiny door in one wall opened onto a narrow passageway containing a ladder that led up to the attic. She climbed up and sat heavily on the floor, her elbows resting on the ledge of a small window. It was a quiet, almost secret place. The others rarely ventured up here. She used it to be on her own, as a place to think.

Far below, men were digging pits at the edge of the trees near the cemetery. Luc was in there somewhere. His mother was right, of course. And now that she had promised, there really was no way out. Yet she recoiled from the idea of rejecting him totally. Why? Because maybe she did love him — maybe she shouldn't turn away from him.

A small framed print hung above the window. It was a picture of the Virgin Mary with a gold halo painted over her head. The gold glowed in the dim attic light. Marie took it down and the Virgin's eyes seemed to move, following her.

Marie knelt and held the painting before her. "What should I do? What can I say to him?" she asked, but Mary would not answer.

Perhaps she was asking the wrong question.

"Is this my home? Am I meant for the church?"

The gold halo sparkled for an instant — Marie blinked. Was that a yes? It must be. The church *was* her home. Or was it? Hélène's song came back to her and with it the thought that perhaps Luc was her heart's love. The same old confusions — the same old doubts. Except she couldn't afford them any longer; there was no more time. She would see Luc tonight before the enemy arrived.

✂ ✂ ✂

Hélène Goyette realized there might be a problem as soon as they drew near the Dakota camp. There were only a couple of lodges and they were in a sad state. Some of the skins were worn through and others were patched with pieces of canvas, even cotton. There was no order to the cooking fires; in fact there was no evidence of an organized camp at all. This meant that there were no women here. It was a shelter for a war party, nothing more. She had planned to introduce herself to the women according to proper manners and ask permission to see the ponies. But no women . . . she hesitated.

A half dozen Dakota men sat outside the largest tent with their backs to her. She did not want to intrude and wasn't sure how to get their attention. A horse and rider approached, branching off the St. Laurent trail that ran past the east end of the camp. A second man walked beside the horse. Both were armed, but both were Cree. Probably coming from One Arrow's Reserve. Here was an opportunity — she waved to them. The rider waved back and veered toward her.

Then he waved again and kicked the horse into a trot. What luck! It was her cousin

Sisbwepew. The other man she recognized as Meitatinas, but she didn't know him very well. Father Moulin's words suddenly came back to her, "renegade savages", and she laughed to herself. Sisebwepew was stubborn, a renegade even, but certainly not a savage. His French was better than hers and he could converse with Dakota, Blackfoot and Englishman alike. He slid easily from the horse and gaped with mock astonishment at the two children.

"*Awas!* We are saved! The Goyette warriors have arrived. Surely now the police will run in fear."

He was a big man with a voice deep as thunder. The musket nestled neatly in the crook of a muscular arm and his beaded leggings gave him a warlike air. The children slunk shyly behind their Mother's skirts.

"Hélène," he smiled. I saw Adrien at the pits yesterday. Never thought he would join Riel."

"We had no option," Hélène replied. "He was shot."

"Yes, I saw the wound." He touched her arm. "I thought of you then. Two of your men fighting. Luc nearly gone at Tourond's Coulee. It must have been difficult."

"Thank you, Sisebwepew." Hélène opened her palms to him. "How are your mother and your wife?"

"In very fine health. They find fault with me though. A man can stand an old woman scolding or a young one — but not both." He winked at Marguerite. "That's why I had to leave and come fight for Riel. The police bullets are kinder to Sisebwepew than his own women!"

"We're not Métis soldiers," Marguerite replied seriously. "But we would like to see the Sioux ponies; they run faster than an eagle flies."

Hélène squeezed her hand.

"Um, we would like to see the ponies PLEASE, *monsieur*."

"Then you will see them, come on."

He led them past the Dakota men. "We are going to look at your fine horses," he called. "The children think Sioux *sunka wankan kinyan*."

"Horses that fly?" one of the Sioux asked, waving his arms like wings. "Compared to your Cree cart horses — they *do* fly!" The other Dakota laughed.

Sisebwepew and Meitatinas returned the laughter but it seemed forced to Hélène. Most of the Métis men had lost their horses to English rifle fire during the fight at Tourond's Coulee.

"What do you make of the Sioux?" she asked quietly.

He frowned. "We fought them and the Blackfoot when I was young. Your people fought them very hard in Montana several times. The Sioux are our enemy I suppose. But this Canadian Army, they are an enemy to everyone. If we lose now, then Métis, Cree, Sioux — all of us — lose forever. So I am happy to have Dakota on my side."

"You trust them then?" Hélène asked. "We heard they left Tourond's battle early."

Sisebwepew stopped walking and faced her. There was anger in his face but he kept it from his voice. "How many men died for Riel at Tourond's, Hélène, do you know?"

She thought for a moment then answered carefully. "Yes, Four. Old Vermette, Pierre Parenteau, . . . "

"No, Hélène," he rumbled. "That is what Riel says — four. There were six. The other two were Dakota Sioux. Left behind by the Métis."

Hélène blushed and lowered her eyes. "I did not know."

Sisebwepew resumed walking. He nudged her and smiled, "Now you do."

They neared the poplar bluff where the ponies were gathered. Marguerite and Jerome ran ahead. "Ho!" Sisebwepew shouted. "Be careful of their wings."

⚒ ⚒ ⚒

Eleazar looped the twine deftly around the log and the stake that supported it. Luc heaved the log up into place and held it while Eleazar snugged it down and tied off the twine. Their pit was over a metre deep and two metres long. Earth was piled high in front of the trench and two stout logs were tied together on top of the earth. Smaller sticks were wedged between the logs so that there was an open slit between them.

Luc jumped into the pit. Crouching slightly he obtained a clear view through the slit. He could shoot from here and be almost completely protected. Moise was placing twigs and leaves over the freshly-dug earth. From a distance their trench was invisible. To his left and right were more trenches situated so that no one could pass through without coming under a Métis gun.

Tonight women from the village would bring up food and ammunition. Then tomorrow . . . He couldn't wait till tomorrow. It might be too late once the fighting started. He climbed out of the pit and set off for the Rectory.

The late afternoon sun hung over the church, just above her cross. Marie stood beyond the church while the children ran to hide. She was supposed to count to one hundred, then go find them, but she lost track of her numbers and her mind wandered again to Luc. How to tell him about her feelings?

The cross cast a long shadow — it reached across the grass toward her. "The truth" it seemed to say, pointing the way. Just tell him the truth. She could not love him, not yet. She needed time to decide — simple and clear. She turned and began walking toward the trenches near the cemetery, resolved to confront her dilemma.

"Hey Marie!" A little voice squealed indignantly from behind the woodpile. They *always* hid behind the woodpile. "Why aren't you hunting for us? Where are you going?"

Marie kept walking and yelled back over her shoulder, "I can't play anymore. You two stay at the rectory; I'll be back in a minute."

"Aw, you promised to play with us." The whiny voices faded as Marie sped up. She had to keep going before she lost her nerve.

Luc descended the ravine to the well at the bottom. He dropped his hat on the grass, rolled up his sleeves and pumped rapidly on the handle. Water gushed out the spout and he sluiced it over his hands then splashed it on his face and scrubbed away the dirt. His shirt-tail served as a towel. He was just retrieving his hat when a figure appeared at the top of the ravine. Marie stood facing the setting sun and waved to him. She seemed to shine in the heavy yellow light.

Marie walked down the ravine and stopped opposite him. She did not speak but her eyes held him steadily. The familiar sensation hit him — like she was a part of him. He was unwilling to make a noise lest he break the spell that had settled on them. Instead he studied her long black hair, plaited down her back, and re-memorized how her cheeks and mouth formed such a kind, beautiful face.

"They will be here tomorrow, the Canadians," she said at last. "So I have to speak to you, now. In a day's time who knows what will become of us."

He nodded mutely, dreading that this might be the end and he would be helpless to prevent it.

"My father and mother serve the Canadians. I have no brother or sister, so I have no family of my own." Her eyes lost their confidence and flickered away from him. She began talking rapidly, gushing like the pump.

"I have come to think of you — the Goyettes — as my family. You are my brother, Luc, and I would do anything for you. I would risk anything for you, because I love you . . . " She stopped, as though surprised by her own words. His heart thumped with anticipation.

"I love you as my brother," she said firmly. "But you don't love me as a sister, do you?"

He stood rigid as her question hit him. Pride flared for a moment, trying to pretend she hadn't hurt him.

"You think we will be together in that church one day, married?"

He found his voice. "Yes Marie, I do. And I won't give you up. We are more than brother and sister. I can feel it, even if you can't."

"There is another family for me, Luc. It has a stronger bond. God is calling to me. I don't know what for yet — I'm confused. Sometimes I think he wants me for himself . . . "

"*Une Soeur?*" Luc burst out. "You'd leave me to be a nun!"

She found herself smiling, calm now that it was in the open. Take vows as a nun — it was a possibility she had scarcely dared to consider. Is that what Mary's picture was trying to tell her?

"Maybe, and maybe not. I'm not certain. That's what I've come to tell you, Luc. Sometimes I also think He wants me to go to you. The truth is that I really don't know what will happen. So for now we are brother and sister."

She took his hands, still damp from the well water. She kissed each one softly and squeezed them tight. Then she turned and ran up the hill. Luc stayed for a long time. The sunlight crept out of the ravine and shadows followed it in. His hands were warm, and tingled from her kiss.

pulled the birdshot, melted it into heavier slugs and repacked them into the shell. These supplies had been safely stored in the pit. Last of all, she prayed for them. They listened, heads bowed, as she spoke.

"Lamb of God who takes away the sin of the world, have mercy on us. Lamb of God who takes away the sin of the world, have mercy on us. Lamb of God who takes away the sin of the world, grant us peace."

They crossed themselves and Eleazar knelt before Hélène. "As the priests refuse to tend us, Madame, will you give us a blessing?"

She hesitated. "It's not my place — it is the priest who should . . . "

"I know, Madame," Moise said. "But better to have your blessing than none at all, before the English come. We beg it of you."

She made the sign of the cross on Moise's forehead and murmured a blessing. She did the same for Eleazar then turned to Luc.

He felt her warm fingertip trace slowly across his face. He thought of their home and all the times she had said bedtime prayers with him. Then she kissed him and took him into her arms. She was trembling.

"God be with you," she whispered in his ear. "My love and my God will be with you, no matter what."

Then she released him and issued a flurry of final instructions on eating and staying dry and being careful. He stared at her, watching her bravery as she picked up the lantern.

"Sleep well, my Luc."

Then she climbed out of the pit and disappeared into the dark. Her lantern bobbed up and down through the trees for a while — then it too disappeared.

It was a dream. Even while he was dreaming, Tom knew that. He knew his eyes were closed and that he lay on the grass in a filthy blanket in a tent on the Saskatchewan prairie. But that didn't matter. He did not want to wake up.

Violet and he were laughing so hard that tears ran down their cheeks. Patrick Flaherty was the cause of their laughter. He stood on their doorstep telling them a story. Tom couldn't quite hear the words but it was funny and outrageous and crazy. It was Paddy.

Tom reached out to take his hand, inviting him into the house but no, he pulled back. His story was finished now and he turned to leave. Violet touched Paddy's sleeve. He looked back over his shoulder at her. The dream froze here.

Paddy's bright and smiling freckled face with the Winnipeg Rifles cap set at a stylish angle over one eye. Violet, dark hair drawn in a thick wave up from her neck. A high spotless lace collar pinned by a brooch whose jewel was nearly as green as her eyes.

Tom dreamed this simple vision. He could make it real, surely, if he dreamed it hard enough.

7
THE NORTHCOTE

Sister Alphonsine shook her head doubtfully. "I don't know, Marie. The English are coming today. Father Moulin wants us to stay close to the house."

Marie cleared the last of the breakfast from the kitchen table and nodded.

"Yes, but they probably won't come this way. Monsieur Goyette says they'll use the Carlton trail and that's a mile away. These little ones will drive me crazy if we stay cooped up inside all day."

Alphonsine frowned. "Where will you be if I give permission?"

"Père said we could do the spring cleanup in the cemetery. You'll be able to see us from here."

Jerome and Marguerite stood quietly — for once — waiting her decision.

"Well, you can go but," the Sister held up a warning hand, "if the soldiers come or any trouble starts . . . "

Marie was already bustling the children out the door. "Then we'll come straight back, Sister."

Marie took the small scythe from the tool shed. She followed Marguerite and Jerome who ran a squealing race to the graveyard. It was set on the high bank overlooking the river. She began cutting back dry, winter-killed grass from the borders of the yard. The two children picked up debris and tidied around the headstones. The sun brought a suggestion of spring. A blue flash darted to a headstone. The bluebird fluttered there for a moment before its mate swooped in and perched beside it. Their blue feathers showed brightly against the grey stone.

Marie read the inscription. *In memory of Ambroise Nolin, beloved father and husband.*

Nolin. Was he Madame Nolin's uncle? At Christmas Father Fourmond had cured Madame Nolin of a terrible illness using holy water brought all the way from Lourdes, France. They said the water came from a creek where the Virgin Mary had appeared to a young girl.

The sudden wail of a riverboat whistle scattered the birds high and away from the headstone. Marie swivelled toward the river where the puffing smoke of a steamer shot upward. The whistle blared again, attracting a mob of heavily armed Métis, Dakota and Cree men who ran past the cemetery and plunged into the trees lining the river. Jerome was almost swept along in their wake but Marie just managed to catch hold of his slippery little hand. He cried and tugged furiously.

"Steamboat Marie! I want to see the steamboat!" His squawking was barely audible above the shriek from the boat's whistle. She glimpsed the smokestacks and pilothouse gliding midstream toward the bend. Then a staccato burst of gunfire came from the Métis.

"Hold still you little *sakimes* — it's too dangerous!" She knelt and clasped him with both arms, praying that Marguerite wouldn't bolt.

The whistle howled sadly now, moving downriver, and it drew the Métis army along with it. Dakota Indians pelted along the shoreline, pausing to fire then racing on to keep up with the boat. Men called to each other, joking and shooting. Their guns popped in a crackling rhythm but they didn't seem to be damaging the big vessel.

It swept around the bend and barked back a few defiant gunshots of its own as it hurried out of sight. Then it was gone, its passing marked by a last string of hysterical hoots. There was an ominous silence in the graveyard. Marie led the children uphill toward the rectory.

Then a new sound came to her, a brief musical lilt. She stopped, and hushed the little ones. There again, a scrap of music on the breeze. Not a fiddle nor a squeezebox. A horn? From the east? Or south? She gazed across the patchwork of bluffs and fields beyond the church. A string of bright red dots, like beads, appeared in the distance then vanished down a ravine. Another red line, much closer, breasted a small rise and stopped. It was joined by a group of dark green figures who quickly extended themselves neatly beside the scarlet.

Soldiers. The Canadians had come, and not by the Carlton trail but right here at the church. The Métis army was scarcely present, most having chased after the boat.

A sudden, desperate urge to be inside the sanctuary of the priests' house seized Marie. Snatching the children's hands she fled.

The riverboat was here! Luc picked up his shotgun and began stuffing shells inside his coat. How could such a huge boat suddenly appear without warning? It was fast — the paddlewheel propelled it rapidly downstream on the current. Luc vaulted from the pit.

"Come on! Before we miss it!" he cried.

Eleazar shook his head. "We'll never run down in time — we're too old and slow. You go Luc, shoot some sailors for us!"

Moise grabbed at the shotgun. "Don't be stupid. Those slugs won't go more than fifty paces accurately." He tossed his own rifle up to Luc. "Here, use this. At least you'll have the range."

He passed Luc a handful of brass cartridges. "Take your time and aim carefully. Don't waste them!"

Luc was already running, pounding through the brush toward the riverbank. Métis men from nearby pits joined him. They burst out of the trees and raced past the cemetery. Marie's anxious face stared from behind a gravestone. There was Jerome, squealing and struggling in Marie's arms. Then Luc hit the next treeline and they were gone. The stream of men veered right and galloped down the steep hill beside the cemetery until they broke clear of the trees.

Luc's heart hammered wildly and he laughed with delight at the excitement of the foot race. They stood on a grassy ledge five metres above the river. The boat was just rounding the sharp bend to their left.

BANG! BANG!

Two rifles exploded together but the boat was still four hundred metres away and the shots seemed puny in the wide river valley.

"*Ekaya! Ekaya!*" Elie Dumont shouted. "Hold your fire, wait until she's opposite."

Luc knelt by a saskatoon bush and raised the rifle. The initials D.B. were carved in tiny letters on the stock. He thought of the policeman who had owned this gun — killed by Moise at Duck Lake last month — and suddenly wished he had his old shotgun. The steamboat whistled again and he pushed the unwanted image from his mind.

It was a fine weapon, with a thick barrel and a smooth breech action. That was all that mattered now. It was heavy for an offhand shot but perfect when he rested his elbow on one knee and tucked the butt into his shoulder. He flipped the breech cover open, inserted one of the large, snub-nosed bullets, slammed the cover shut and cocked the hammer.

A half dozen Cree from One Arrow's reserve crashed through the trees behind him.

"*Kipa* brothers!" Elie greeted them. "You are just in time."

The boat's lower deck was well protected by planks and oat bags but the upper deck and the pilothouse were bare. The boat's name was printed clearly on the bow, *Northcote*. Luc steadied his rifle sight on the pilot's open window. The faces of two men were visible in the opening as it glided past, only a hundred metres away. He squeezed the trigger; the gun bucked back hard and belched a small cloud of smoke. A large splinter of wood flew from the window ledge and the men dropped out of sight. The One Arrow warriors opened fire — a dozen more shots punctured the pilothouse and smacked into the upper deck.

"YIP — YIP!" Luc barked like a coyote over a kill as he fumbled for another cartridge.

They loaded and fired as fast as they could — but the big steamer sailed majestically past them.

"Come on, *Waniska!*" Elie shouted, and he ran along the bank. Luc followed him, dodging along the winding path, shouting insults at the soldiers on the boat and cheering his friends. They sprinted down the river until they were ahead of the boat then opened fire again.

Luc's gun ate his last three shells then fell silent. If only Moise had given him a few more. The others continued to pound the ship until it pulled out of range. They ran again to chase it but Luc climbed the bank and went to the road that connected Batoche with the church. By the time he returned to Moise, begged more bullets and got back, the boat would be long gone. So he turned right and began trudging up the ridge. The rectory roof was just visible above the crest. All the excitement of the riverboat had drained away; his shoulders sagged under the weight of the gun.

He just reached the upper plateau when a half dozen men came into view, running past the rectory along the trail toward him. The leader looked like Eleazar. Something was wrong. Why weren't they in their trenches? He jogged forward to meet them.

"What is it? Where are you going?"

Moise, Eleazar and the others barely slowed down.

"Go, Luc! Warn Dumont to bring the men back." Eleazar bellowed. "The English are here — on the Humboldt trail."

Luc tried to stop them. "But our trenches? Should we go back to our pit and try to hold them off?"

Moise snatched his rifle from Luc. He thrust the shotgun into Luc's hands and shoved him back down the trail to Batoche.

"They're all over the cemetery! Hundreds of them. They have overrun our pits, you young fool!" he gasped. "Now run and get Dumont or all is lost!"

The nine-pound shell punched right through the walls of the wood house. The gunners reloaded the cannon and slammed another shell into the building. This one exploded with a crash that blew out the windows. A moment later smoke billowed from under the eaves.

"If there were any rebels sheltering there . . . well, they're gone now," Lt. Alderson said. G Company stood in three ranks while the guns were taken out of action and hooked up to their limbers and horse teams. Then the column resumed its march along the trail skirting the river. By the time they passed the house it was burning fiercely. The *Northcote*'s whistle wailed faintly in the distance, barely audible above the crackle of flames.

Beyond the house were two more buildings, nearly a kilometre away. One was white and large, like a church. They must be near Batoche, Tom thought. Where were the enemy? Had they run without a fight? He felt strangely let down — cheated. They had to fight. How could he avenge Paddy without a fight?

The army must have read Tom's mind for seconds later it changed into its fighting formation. The Winnipeg battalion marched into a field on the left and lined up at a right angle to the road. The 10th Grenadiers did the same thing on the right side of the road. Like a door swinging open on its hinge, the front of the army transformed itself from a narrow, winding column to a long, straight battle line.

"Well Tom, looks like front rank for us again," Jim said pointing back down the trail. The General's aide was holding the Midland men on the road while the General led the Royal Grenadiers to the right.

"Winnipeg left — Toronto right, and Midland gets to be the reserve. Lucky beggars."

"Maybe we're the lucky ones," Tom said. "What if the rebels run? We might be the only ones to get a chance at them."

"Aye, could be you're right." The Sergeant Major nodded. "Or could be they'll fight and we will have more cause for revenge, if that's what you mean."

Tom felt the sting of his uncle's comment but showed nothing.

"Because if we're only fighting for revenge that's what happens, eh? You never get even. You kill some of them, then they kill some of us, so we go back at them — never stop fighting."

Tom looked away. His uncle was his anchor — his reminder of home. But Paddy's death had pushed a wedge between them and it seemed to be widening.

"What's the plan, Sergeant Major?" Walt called from the ranks behind them. "G Company first for the Glory again?" The men laughed nervously.

"Here's an idea, sir. Why not let the Midlanders put in the assault and we'll follow 'em. So we don't hog all the credit."

"Better yet," Alex piped up. "You surrender, Walt. Then in about two days yon rebels will be oot of food cause you will have scarfed all of it, and they'll have to quit or starve."

The men hooted at Walt's red face.

"Shut up, you Scotch git!" He roared. "The Sergeant Major and I were discussing high strategy — not for the likes of Glasgow gutter sweepings who — "

"G Company!" Lieutenant Alderson cut the debate short. "Atten . . . shun!"

The laughter died and the men steadied up as General Middleton and his staff officers cantered toward them. Alderson whipped his sword out, nearly fumbled it, then managed to salute smartly.

"As you were, Lieutenant," the General called genially. "Glad to see your men are in such good spirits. What company is this?"

"G C,C,C . . . um, G Company," Alderson said. "G Company, this is, ah, sir."

The general and his aide exchanged an embarrassed look.

"THE LITTLE BLACK DEVILS, General!" A huge, confident voice bellowed from the ranks. It was Snell, red faced and wild eyed. "Just point us to the rebels, sir!"

The company cheered loudly and the General beamed. "Steady lads, all in good time." He brushed the tips of his long white moustaches, then pointed over his shoulder to the buildings.

"Yonder is the Catholic mission outside Batoche. In a few moments we'll visit Johnny Rebel and I hope the men from G Company will be steadfast on my left flank." His brisk British accent was reassuring. He might be grey haired and tubby, Tom thought, but he was a real soldier.

"Will you do that for me my lads?"

The men howled, no more nervous worries. Alderson stuck his cap on the tip of his sword and waved it in the air. A thrill prickled up and down Tom's spine. By heavens, they'd hit those rebels hard this time!

"Elie!" Luc screamed, then sucked in a huge lungful of air. "They are here! In the cemetery — the church . . . " He gasped, unable to get any more out. He stumbled but quickly regained his footing. He sprinted toward the Métis men where they had gathered on the riverbank to take long shots at the disappearing riverboat.

Elie Dumont turned. "What? What is it?"

"Soldiers!" Luc shrieked. "At the church!"

Even at that distance Luc could see the shock of surprise on Elie's face. Then the Métis army began running toward the hill where their church and rectory were being invaded.

⚒ ⚒ ⚒

The line of Winnipeg riflemen moved like a green wave through the grass towards the trees. The wave rippled and swayed as it swept through the bluff. Lieutenant Alderson glanced nervously over his shoulder, checking that he was still positioned in front of G Company as the men crashed through the brush.

The trees held a special threatening quality. They sheltered Métis rebels and invisible guns that killed without warning. Tom's eagerness to meet the rebels eroded with every step. He flinched at the sound of a branch snapping and surged forward, anxious to get back to the sunlight. He burst onto an open pasture a moment later.

To the left a picket fence enclosed a cluster of crosses overlooking the river. To the right were the two buildings; one was a whitewashed church and the other a two-story house. Between the graveyard and the buildings the ground dropped into a heavily wooded ravine and beyond it an open plateau overlooked the river valley. The dark woods and deep gully were identical to the coulee at Fish Creek. Tom stopped, suddenly unsure of himself. Lieutenant Alderson passed him and turned around, holding his sword up like a policeman's baton.

"Form here, G Company! Reform on this line!"

The green ripple emerged from the trees and reshaped itself into a solid line. Then it stopped and rested. Tom stretched out full length in the thick grass and propped his head up on one hand. Uncle Jim sat beside him, smoking a pipe. A breeze fluttered the ribbons on the back of Tom's cap. They tickled his neck where the morning sunlight warmed his skin. Neither spoke but it felt good to have his uncle beside him again and Tom's mind drifted to home. What were his father and Vi doing this morning? Winnipeg seemed like a different world.

The thump of horse's hooves interrupted his daydream; Major Mckeand rode toward them. Lieutenant Alderson jumped to his feet and Tom went to his side.

"Right then, Alderson. Here's the plan," Mckeand said, leaning down from his horse and pointing toward the ravine. "The General is going to take Boulton's men and the Grenadiers to push on past the church toward the village. But first he wants the artillery to secure the far side of the coulee while we hold this side."

The young Lieutenant breathed loudly, as though he had just run a mile, but he kept his face calm.

"Take your company and line them up along the ravine," Mckeand continued. "I'll spread the rest of the battalion out behind you and into the cemetery. Understood?"

Alderson swallowed and nodded again. "This — ah — you mean right here. Um . . . this side, sir?" He pointed vaguely.

"That's it," Mckeand swung his horse around and trotted off. "Carry on, Lieutenant."

Tom stood by the silent young officer, listening to the hoarse, nervous breathing. He fidgeted and cleared his throat but Alderson remained immobile.

"Sir?" Tom tried quietly. "Are you alright?"

Alderson twitched.

"G Company!" he shrilled. "Attention!"

The men climbed to their feet, waiting expectantly for his orders.

Alderson's hand fiddled with his sword belt and he coughed, but said nothing. A snicker came from the ranks and voices began to mutter. *Don't freeze now.* Tom cringed. *Not on your first battlefield assignment.*

"Sir," he whispered. "Just get them moving, say something."

"Follow me!" The words popped from Alderson and startled Tom with their force. Then the Lieutenant turned and marched for the ravine. G Company, expecting a more formal set of commands wobbled in confusion. Some men began talking and broke ranks.

"You heard the Company Commander!" Sergeant Major Kerslake roared. "Dress off *me* — keep your ranks — get moving!"

Miraculously the confusion evaporated and G Company swung off in pursuit of their officer who was already near the coulee. Tom followed with them, waiting for rebel gunfire to pour out of the ravine into Alderson. Surely the rebels wouldn't leave such a strong place undefended?

It was empty. Except for a water well pump.

As the men arrived, Lieutenant Alderson waved them into position. One rank on the edge of the coulee and the second rank slightly back, covering the first. He led them to their positions, running to and fro checking their alignment. His earlier nerves had mysteriously vanished.

Sergeant Major Kerslake stood back watching. A huge grin creased his face. "Well Tom, our officer may not be much for the drill manual, but he can build a firing line in short order. Give him a real job and leave the strutting on a parade square to the others, eh?"

Alderson darted up and down the line, pausing to fling himself to the ground to check each soldier's aiming points. He was a new man, Tom thought.

"Sergeant Major, look here." Walt and Alex were taking up their post in the second line but something in the trees behind them had caught their attention. It was a log — half buried in the earth. Behind the log was a deep trench. A sick feeling flushed Tom's stomach. A Métis rifle pit, so well hidden they had walked right past it.

"Another one! There, just inside the trees in the gully!" Alex pointed.

Tom gazed into the pit. If the rebels had been at their posts, G Company would have been shot to pieces. Why had they abandoned their forts without a fight?

Gabriel Dumont was furious. "My God! Redcoats on the mission hill already!"

The Métis army was huddled in a confused crowd in the trees at the bottom of the high ridge crowned by the Catholic Mission. A line of Boulton's men appeared at the crest and a hint of panic swept through the Métis. Luc felt it grip him. Was it over, then? The enemy cannon could smash Batoche from the hilltop. Would they have to surrender without a fight?

"Children!" Eleazar's voice cackled. "Don't wet your pants. It's easy! If the Englishmen are on the hill — then we'll just shoot them off it."

"The crazy old man is right," Gabriel snapped. "The redcoats are on the open skyline. We can hide in the trees below, like at Tourond's. But we must move now, quickly. Elie!"

Elie Dumont came to his brother.

"Take your men and get into the bottom of the coulee. Work your way through the trees until you are behind those Englishmen on the plateau, then open fire. I'll take the others and circle in to the rear of the rectory. We'll have them like a muskrat in a trap. That should keep them out of Batoche!"

Elie called for his men. Luc raced after him, wishing he still had Moise's rifle instead of the old shotgun. His father loped along at his side, dodging trees and glancing up toward the mission.

8
MISSION RIDGE

Tom crouched with his uncle in the enemy trench, peering through the slit in the logs. Lieutenant Alderson stood beside them.

"Well sited and perfectly hidden," Jim said with a tone of grudging admiration. "I'm glad we didn't have to take it by frontal assault."

"Amen to that, Sergeant Major," Alderson said. "Doesn't bear thinking about." He looked back over the open pasture they had crossed on the far side of the trees. "But we've been lucky. Seems like we may get into Batoche without a fight." He pointed toward the house and church. "I wager they're happy it's over."

A group of civilians, two in long black robes — priests — were milling around the entrance to the house. The General's heavyset figure was in the centre of the crowd. One of the priests was gesturing down the trail across the plateau. He seemed to be shouting at the General. A crow squawked loudly from the trees in the ravine below them. Tom smiled. The black cawing crow and the black-robed priest could have been brothers.

The gunfire erupted all at once. No warning shots, no chance to prepare themselves. Just a long rip of crackling shots from beyond the house.

"Boulton's men have caught the opening packet again," Jim muttered. "Poor devils."

The din of rifle fire increased and extended itself like a drum roll.

"There g-g-g-go the 10th Royals!" Lieutenant Alderson's excited voice rose over the noise. He ran to the edge of the coulee and waved his cap, shouting across the ravine toward the Toronto soldiers. "Hurrah the Grenadiers!"

Tom glanced at his uncle in surprise. "What's got into him, Sergeant Major? He's afraid to give an order on parade but when we find the rebels he goes crazy!"

"Like I said before, Tom," his uncle chuckled, "he's not much on the drill square but he looks like he might make a dandy soldier."

Two companies of scarlet coats had spread themselves into four parallel ranks in front of the priests' house. Then bugles began calling and the lines swept out onto the plateau, cheering loudly. The rebel fire turned to thunder and one of the Grenadiers flopped forward on his face. The rest marched over the crest and went down out of sight.

Lieutenant Alderson paced like a caged dog back and forth along the G Company line, craning his neck to see the battle. He stopped to talk with Snell and the two of them laughed as though they were the best of friends. Some of the men left their positions to join him, pointing toward the plateau. Two cannons galloped out behind the Grenadiers spraying dust as the horses wheeled sharply to swing the great guns into position. Less than a minute later the first shot boomed.

Alderson ran to the rifle pit. "Sergeant Major! Here, quickly Sergeant Major." His face was flushed. "They need our help. I'm going to ask the CO for permission to take our company in with the Grenadiers."

"With respect," Jim answered quietly, "he won't let you go. If they need help there's still two more Grenadier companies and all the Midlanders. Our job is to protect their flank —

keep rebels from coming up the gully behind them."

"But it's empty!" Alderson snapped impatiently. "We're wasting our time here."

"I agree." Tom climbed out of the pit and joined the lieutenant. "We might miss our chance if we don't get in now."

Jim turned his Sergeant Major stern-faced glare on him. "Buglers do not make decisions or offer opinions in this army."

Tom flinched.

"You should know better, Bugler Kerslake."

Teeth clenched in embarrassment, Tom looked to Alderson for support. The young officer adjusted his sword belt and coughed self-consciously.

"Naturally you're right, CSM. One can't disobey orders." He wandered to the edge of the ravine and peered into the tangle of bare trees at the bottom. "Still, it seems unfair we are stuck here with nothing to do. I wonder if that well has good water. We should refill our bottles while it's quiet."

The tip of a poplar twig whipped across Luc's cheek. It laid a deep scratch in the flesh but he scarcely noticed it as he crawled through the underbrush. He paused for a moment and looked up cautiously. They were perhaps ten metres from the edge of the woods. He could just make out the pump handle on the well beyond the trees.

"Father," he whispered. "The well." Then he pointed to the top of the coulee. "Our pit is just over there.

Adrien was on his knees and elbows to Luc's right. He raised his arm to signal the others — they halted. Gunfire from Gabriel's men at the rectory had nearly ceased. An English voice came clearly from the top of the ravine.

"Sergeant Major," it shouted. "Detail some men to collect all the water bottles."

Luc's heart raced into a wild, pounding pace. The enemy were right here! He sank flat to the earth, burrowing into the carpet of dead leaves. A sharp metallic click sounded. Father had cocked his rifle and was aiming upwards. A tall, thin soldier stood on the edge. His dark green uniform looked new and expensive. He was young, almost a boy, and he held a sword in his right hand.

WHAM

Adrien's shot catapulted the young man backwards in a somersault. Métis rifles barked from the trees. Somebody screamed a war cry — Luc recognized his own voice. The war cry had come from a part of him that he no longer controlled. The hair on the back of his neck prickled as he pulled his shotgun up to his shoulder. A row of Canadians popped up above the rim of the coulee, all wearing the black tunics and funny narrow caps. He knew them from Tourond's — The Little Black Devils. He thrust his shotgun forward and pulled both triggers.

Lieutenant Alderson's long thin legs seemed to take flight at the same instant the shot sounded. His feet kicked high in the air and he landed heavily on his back. His pant leg was torn lengthwise from the knee to the thigh and a blood-red streak shone through the tear. He sat up and stared stupidly at the wound. Then he struggled to his feet and limped to where his cap and sword had fallen in the grass.

"NO!" Tom called. "GET BACK!"

Alderson stooped, picked up his cap and placed it on his head, adjusting it to sit just right. Then he retrieved his sword and put it back in his scabbard. G Company rifles began to reply to the rebels and a wild chanting cry came from the trees at the bottom of the ravine.

"Steady lads," Sergeant Major Kerslake shouted cheerfully. "Fire low into the tree line, boys — give 'em hell!"

He walked calmly to Alderson's side and dusted bits of grass from his uniform.

"JIM!" Tom cried. "Come back!"

Uncle Jim placed one hand on the officer's shoulder. "Bad one, sir?" he asked politely.

Were they both crazy, standing at the edge in full view? Tom's vision blurred. Was this some kind of sick nightmare?

"Oh no. Must have been the extreme angle — funny actually but the bullet barely broke the skin. Just a scratch, hardly deep enough to draw blood." Alderson smiled. "Trousers are ruined though, bad luck."

That was it; they were both insane. Tom leaped to his feet and ran at them. He'd lost Paddy like this — he'd rather die than lose his uncle.

"Ah . . . the Bugler seems upset," Alderson said.

"He's right actually," Jim replied. "We'd best get behind the firing line."

Tom grabbed his uncle's arm and ran him away from the deadly ground. Alderson joined them but he refused to stay still. Soon he was pacing behind the line urging the men to fight hard. At the rectory, stretcher bearers were carrying two Grenadier casualties in through the front door.

Heavy hobnailed boots clumped everywhere. Heavy Englishmen's voices murmured in pain, shouted orders, swore and laughed, filling the rectory where before only nuns and priests had spoken. Heavy cannon thunder right outside the rectory; heavy hail occasionally hammered the clapboards throwing splinters inside as bullets pierced the walls. A gasping soldier boy, scarlet tunic soaked with dark blood, clutched at Marie's hand. Mistaking her for a nun, he begged a prayer. Marie couldn't refuse — enemy or not. She began to pray.

"In English! I don't understand French. Please, in English," he wheezed.

She recommenced. "Hail Mary, full of Grace, the Lord is with thee. Blessed art thou among women." He must be Protestant, did they say Hail Mary? Too bad if they didn't; they were the only English words she could think of right now.

"And blessed is the fruit of thy womb, Jesus."

His grip slackened. She squeezed her eyes shut, afraid she was doing a priest's job and yet afraid not to in case this boy should die without a prayer.

"Holy Mary, Mother of God, pray for us sinners now and at the hour of our death."

She made the sign of the cross and touched her silver Mary. The soldier's hand dropped away; she couldn't open her eyes to watch his death.

"Thank you, thank you very much. Ah . . . *merci beaucoup, mademoiselle.*"

She opened, and saw his smile of gratitude.

Then cut more bandages, make more tea, and check on the children in the cellar. Marguerite is gone — then found — in the front room chatting to an officer wearing a dark green uniform. He speaks French to Marguerite and gives her peppermint. She squeals, "*Merci, merci!*". Outside, more gunfire, Adrien and Luc trying to kill the Green officer's boys — the soldiers trying to kill her Luc. More heavy boots, more sour-smelling casualties packing into the rectory, trampling it down and filling it with tobacco smoke.

⚔ ⚔ ⚔

"Luc — there!" Adrien roared, fumbling to reload his rifle and pointing to the left. A soldier stood on the hilltop drawing his rifle up. He wore a blue tunic and white belt. Long sideburn whiskers and curly dark hair straggled from under his tuque. Luc rose to his knees and lifted his shotgun in slow motion, even though his father screamed to hurry. The blue soldier was already aiming, his rifle seemed to grow twenty metres long, its muzzle reaching through the trees for Luc's heart.

Luc knew he'd lost. Even as the shotgun's butt slid up against his shoulder he saw the enemy's finger twitch in the trigger guard. Then came a sudden spurt of English smoke that he was too late to avoid.

SNAP!

The noise seemed to come from within his ear, but it was the enemy bullet breaking air a millimetre from his head. The Canadian watched for him to fall. Luc's shotgun exploded and the tuque jumped. A head full of curly hair whipped back then sank from view. A moment later the blue body rolled down the hillside, coming to rest against a tree not ten metres away. One forearm was tucked under his head, just the same way that little Jerome slept. The white belt and blue cloth were strangely pretty among the grey, bare trees. The soldier's legs kicked twice as though stung by a wasp, then fell horribly limp.

Luc sat back and with trembling fingers reloaded his gun. Mother's words raced through his mind. "Lamb of God who takes away the sin of the world, have mercy on us." But he couldn't tear his eyes away from the terrible, misshapen bundle of blue cloth and curly dark hair.

"The artillery have a wounded man farther down the coulee," Lieutenant Alderson explained. "We will charge with the Midlanders down past the well into the trees to create a diversion. Then the gunners will retrieve their man. Any questions?"

G Company's corporals were gathered around their company commander near the abandoned enemy rifle pit.

"How do we know when the diversion is over?" Snell asked.

"The artillery trumpeters will sound the retire; Bugler Kerslake will repeat it. When you hear that bugle call, get your men out of the ravine. We'll reform here, by this pit."

There were no other questions. The NCOs returned to their men, shouting orders to form ranks. G Company rose up from the earth and moved away from the edge of the coulee. A moment's shuffling built its assault formation then G Company tensed itself to spring. Tom checked his bugle for the hundredth time to ensure it was clean.

Opposite them the Midlanders formed a line that suddenly swept down into the gully, firing as they went like a red engine puffing smoke.

"Bugler — " Alderson was cut short by Tom's horn. It leaped to his mouth and blared the advance. Walt, crimson with sweat and Alex, white with fear, strode past him. The green line belched its fire into the trees.

"Steady men! K-K-Keep your line! Rapid fire, lively now." Lieutenant Alderson's redundant commands filtered through the ripping battle noise as the Winnipeg Rifles entered the deadly forest. Tom's hunger for revenge swelled up — he longed to satisfy it. Surely this time he'd see a dead rebel to atone for Paddy.

Red coats on the left and above, green uniforms on the right, brightly-coloured soldiers everywhere. No longer single shots but a steady flow of rifles spewing smoke into the bush. Luc's legs took him of their own will and raced him back through the trees away from the multicoloured, smoking monster. Métis men flitted through the woods beside him, dodging and weaving as English bullets chased them in a deadly game of hide and seek.

Suddenly a Métis head popped up from beneath his feet. Then another and another emerged from the earth. It was the second line of rifle pits below Mission Ridge and Elie's men were in them. Luc kept running, certain Elie couldn't break the wave of soldiers. A Métis volley erupted from the pits. The English voices shouted in confusion. A trumpet called a stuttering tune and the shooting storm subsided. Farther back another bugle took up the song but it seemed almost reluctant.

❦ ❦ ❦

"Sound the recall!" Alderson had Tom by the arm and shook him.

Tom plucked at the bugle's mouthpiece and pretended to fumble it, letting it drop. Then he knelt slowly. He couldn't blow the retreat, not yet. He had to stall. The rebels would run — they were almost broken. The Winnipeg Rifles had to press harder, kill them while they were out of their trenches.

"RECALL NOW!" The young Lieutenant bellowed to the men closest. His torn trousers fluttered in the breeze revealing the red gash underneath. "RETIRE! PULL BACK G!"

The CSM repeated the command from the bush to their right. Men were stopping, firing a last poorly-aimed shot, then backing away from the Métis pits. The artillery trumpeter farther up the ravine was sounding the recall clearly. Tom retrieved the mouthpiece and replaced it in the horn. What a chance they had! Now it was ruined — no atonement — no revenge. His frustration swelled up and he kicked a rotten tree stump.

"Sound the Retire, smartly n-n-n . . . ah, right now, bugler!" Alderson commanded.

Tom raised the bugle and blew angrily, hoping G Company would not listen. But they did. Like well-trained hunting dogs the Company backed up through the woods and regrouped on top of the ravine. Jim counted them all present. There had not been a single rebel casualty in the trees and that was intolerable; Tom's gut twisted with rage.

The other companies of the 90th Battalion were leaving the cemetery. Cannon were hooking up to their limbers and horses near the church. A long quiet descended over the battlefield. Stretchers bearing wounded soldiers flowed out of the priests' house and into two waiting wagons. The last stretcher carried an artilleryman in blue coat and white belt. His head and shoulders were covered by a blanket.

"Wasted our time down in the coulee, eh?"

"What?" Tom was startled by Corporal Snell's appearance at his side. "Wasted our time?"

"Yup. The wounded gunner," Snell pointed at the last stretcher. "That's him, dead, not wounded at all. We charged the ravine to rescue a dead man." He laughed harshly. "Well, I've had enough of this for one day. My belly is grumbling — got anything to eat, Kerslake?"

The angry coals in Tom's stomach felt as though they had just been fanned by a bellows.

"EAT? FOOD!" Tom snapped.

Snell bristled. "That's what I said, bugler, and watch your damned insubordinate tongue!"

"But Corporal," Tom checked his anger and appealed to Snell's instincts. "We should be back down there, killing those vermin. Look what they've done to us! Wagons full of wounded and dead. We're just supposed to take it and go home for supper?"

"Sounds good to me," Walt strolled up. "Any grub going, Corp? Little Kerslake? You must have something to eat, eh?"

It was too much! What was wrong with them? Tom's anger overflowed and he lost control. He fished a biscuit out of his haversack and threw it at Walt. "There's your precious grub," he snarled.

"Maybe if you shot as well as you eat we'd have repaid them for Paddy instead of — "

"Watch yourself, sonny," Walt took two quick steps and slammed his heavy paw against Tom's chest, knocking him backwards. "I've done my duty this day by God! I'll have words right now with anyone who says different!"

Tom shook with helpless rage.

"Bugler Kerslake!" Lieutenant Alderson's voice called from near the ravine. "Where is that boy?"

"Ah, there you are. Come along, look sharp now. The army is falling back, Winnipeg is covering the retreat."

The wagons were already moving and red lines of Grenadiers were marching away from Batoche. The crow had returned to the coulee, cawing and laughing at them. Otherwise the battlefield was quiet.

The setting sun threw long sharp shadows in front of the Métis as they cautiously climbed to the crest of Mission Ridge. The open plateau was littered with the debris of battle. Clothing, shell cases, smashed cartridge boxes and the stiffening corpses of two dead horses. Their glazed, staring eyes saddened Luc. One was a fine grey gelding still wearing its harness. The soldiers had cut its traces to free the team.

"There they go!" Gabriel Dumont's gleeful shout rallied his little army. "Let's send them on their way with a Métis farewell."

He knelt and fired *Le Petit*. The line of Canadians was over a half kilometre away, far on the other side of the church, but Gabriel's long shot of defiance cheered the men. With a singing war cry they roused themselves for one last effort and trotted after their leader to chase the enemy off Métis land.

But one young warrior did not follow the victory. Luc ran to the rectory, afraid that Marie would be gone, terrified that she and the children had been taken by the English. The door stood open and he leaped up the stairs, through the entry hall and into the kitchen.

"Luc!" Marguerite shot out from behind the table and launched herself into his arms. "The soldiers were here! Look, look, peppermints." She clutched a white candy stick in her chubby hand. "You can lick one but don't eat it 'cause it's mine."

She thrust the peppermint into his face. He licked the sweet and hugged her.

"Where are Jerome and Marie?"

"Uh oh," her smile drooped. "They're in the cellar — I'm supposed to be with them but I sneaked up here to see the soldiers leave."

"Marguerite you disobedient little *gosse* . . ." Marie appeared in the doorway with Jerome. Luc met her eyes. She kissed her small, silver Mary figure.

"Thank God, Luc. Thank God you're alright," she whispered. Her eyes held him but she made no move toward him.

"I was afraid you had gone with the priests to the enemy camp," he replied.

"Father Moulin? Fourmond? They are upstairs," she bristled, defending her priests. "Why would they go to the English?"

"Gabriel says they betrayed us — helped the enemy," he snapped back.

"We tended to injured men and prayed over their dead," she said. "If that is treason, then I am a traitor too. I thought we were just being Christians."

"I'm sorry, Marie, I didn't mean it like that." It sounded lame, even to him. Her face was set in anger. "You know I'm loyal to the church, ah . . . " He ran out of words and stood tongue-tied, wishing for some way to change the subject. He didn't care about the priests — he'd come to see her and the children but somehow they were arguing over the church again.

"Are you hungry?" she asked, finally.

He grinned. "Starving! The English took my pit this morning so I've had nothing to eat all day."

"Come on then," she smiled back at him. "If I can feed the Canadians I guess I can feed the rebels too. Or do you have to get Gabriel's permission first?"

He laughed. Friends, he thought. At least we're still friends.

The wagons were circled end to end, enclosing a ten acre patch of pasture that included two small sloughs. Outside the wall of wagons, the soldiers dug.

Tom jabbed his bayonet into the ground and pried out a lump of dirt. Alex scooped it onto a tin plate and threw it out of the trench. They'd been working nearly two hours and had scratched down only a half metre.

BANG! POP!

Two flashes sparkled in the dark treeline at the river's edge two hundred metres away. Tom and Alex flopped down in their little shelter as one of the bullets buzzed high overhead. Tom's anger was long gone — replaced by hunger, exhaustion and a thirst that was choking him. More than fourteen hours of marching, running, fighting and digging with only a cup of tea and a chunk of salt pork for breakfast.

His uncle appeared out of the twilight.

"Right lads — come on in, B Company will take over."

"Oh gosh, Sergeant Major," Walt called loudly. "Do we HAVE to quit so soon? I want to keep on digging and being shot at. Please don't make me stop for supper."

The other men were so weary they didn't even laugh in their rush to leave the trenches. A cluster of cooking fires twinkled in the centre of the Zareba, not far from two tents that served as a field hospital. Tom joined the queue of hungry soldiers. He received a biscuit, a small piece of pork and a cup of scalding tea. The tea was bitter and there was no sugar but he didn't care. He dunked the hardtack into his cup then chewed and drank rapidly. He didn't dare sit down; he was so worn out he wouldn't have the strength to stand up again.

"Bet you regret throwing your tack at me, eh?"

Walt joined him by the fire.

"I owe you an apology." Tom's cheeks burned with embarrassment. "I never meant to question your courage, Walt."

"Yup, it was Patrick Flaherty at the bottom of your anger I'm guessing," Walt said gently. "He's gone, boy. And like your uncle says, shooting a barn full of half-breeds won't change things. We'll whip 'em soon enough and we'll knock a few of them over when we do. I say good riddance. BUT, I'm not thinking you can trade one of them for Paddy. You can't pay him off."

Walt was speaking plain, common sense. Yet part of Tom still wanted revenge. He was still hungry to take a life back — a debt was owed. He couldn't bear another argument with Walt, so he stayed quiet.

"Preacher's going to say a few words in a minute," Walt nudged him. "Maybe you could talk it all over with him, after the service. Can't

187

hurt, eh? Reverend Gordon's a decent fellow and he's a Winnipeg man — he'll understand."

Walt's mention of a Winnipeg minister sparked a flash of memories. Father and Vi every Sunday — best clothes — the big Anglican Church — the boring sermons — Violet's one day of perfume. Every Sunday Vi's triumph — roast, gravy, puddings crackling, potatoes — then Jim and Father with pipes and port wine — boring discussions on farm prices, homesteading and Winnipeg politics. Oh for such a day now, to be bored and well fed and at home. Maybe a Winnipeg preacher could bring Violet and Father back for a moment and make everything . . . normal again.

They crossed the Zareba and joined a mixed group of men from all the Regiments. They were clustered in a large semicircle around a lantern set on top of a crate.

"Gentlemen." Reverend Gordon called for their attention. "I propose to say just a few words if our friends yonder will permit."

As if on cue a rebel bullet smacked into the wagon box behind them. The minister smiled and a nervous laugh shot through the congregation.

"As you know, we lost two of our comrades today. Gunner Phillips of A Battery and Private Moore of the 10th Royal Grenadiers. As well, many others lie seriously wounded. I would ask you to bow your heads in prayer for them. O Lord, hear now . . . "

Tom thought of Paddy's burial and squeezed his eyes shut. The soothing words poured into him. He was desperate for them to relieve his pains.

" . . . gallant young men who have paid the supreme price. You have called them from our ranks to stand at your side, Father. Though their mothers and families may grieve for them, yea we know they are now in paradise with . . . "

Paradise? Tom tried to put Paddy there but he couldn't picture it. He could remember Paddy calling out for his mother after the rebel bullet thumped into him. He could imagine Paddy's mother writing him a letter after he was already dead — then crying for him. But he couldn't see Paddy in paradise, not yet, not until he had been avenged.

" . . . close this brief service by reciting the words God gave us. Our Father, which art in heaven. Hallowed be thy name. Thy kingdom come, thy will be done . . . "

Tom recited the prayer through clenched teeth. It was no good. This preacher could not conjure Violet or Father, nor could he take the pain away and put Paddy to rest. Only revenge could do that, even if the others couldn't understand it. So Tom Kerslake prayed for a chance to take that revenge in tomorrow's battle.

Jerome and Marguerite slept softly on either side of Marie. She shifted to a more comfortable spot on the straw-filled mattress but they didn't stir. Exhausted by the day's events she wanted to sleep as well but she couldn't. Their mattress lay on the floor of the small post office on the second story of the rectory. The nuns were downstairs — Sister Alphonsine's snoring carried up to her but that wasn't the problem. It was Luc and her old dilemma. She had nearly run after him when he left this evening. Something held her back and it had to do with the nuns, the church, her cross and her silver Mary. They called her home more strongly than her feelings for Luc called her to leave. Didn't they?

She sat up and stared out the gable window at the stars in the south sky. An occasional gunshot came faintly from the east where the Dakota were sniping at the Canadian camp. Luc and the Métis had returned to their rifle pits to eat, gather ammunition and rest. What if tomorrow was Luc's turn to be carried into the Rectory — like the wounded Englishmen had been today? What would she do?

The front door rattled, then creaked open. The soft pad of moccasin-feet rippled across the floorboards. Moccasins, not boots, and without any warning or greeting shouted first. Trouble, maybe as bad as the English trouble, had just arrived downstairs. Instinctively she grabbed the children's hands.

A dozen muffled voices seeped through the planks to her. Some of them were French, some Cree. Père Caribou's voice rose above the confused babel; it was angry. "Oh Père," she whispered. "Don't lose your temper. These men are dangerous tonight."

"It is no longer your authority that rules here, Father Moulin." A clear and very calm voice restored order. "Our people looked to you once, but not now." It was Louis Riel.

"That!" Moulin's voice hoarsely shot back, "that is pure blasphemy! Neither of us rules — God rules in this house. How dare you invade this rectory with your guns?"

"What!" Riel exclaimed. "How is this different from the English soldiers you welcomed this morning? You fed and tended and for all I know prayed over them." Marie cringed at the memory of her prayer for the wounded redcoat. "While your own people — the Métis who once loved you — fought and bled for Batoche without so much as a thought from their so-called priests."

"You forbade us from entering Batoche!" Moulin screeched in frustration.

"Of course I did. To avoid just such a betrayal as you have committed." There was anger now in Riel's tone. "I did not ask to be God's representative. The role fell on my shoulders. God called me when he saw your face turned against him."

"Enough! Get out! OUT! I say," Père Caribou grunted. Feet thumped loudly and furniture crashed.

"NO! Always you betray us, Priest!" Dumont's sudden bellow shook the rectory. The children jumped, wide eyed. Marie motioned for them to be quiet. "We saw soldiers here, thick as fleas on a dog's back, during the fight." A rifle lever crunched loudly as it was cocked. "Traitor! Where are they?"

Moulin yapped back a denial, daring them to search the house. Then a surge of threats and boasts spilled from the battle-excited men. Marie looked for a place to hide. The attic? — no time! The large cupboard under the post office counter. She rushed the children from their bed and all three squeezed in. She wasn't even sure why she was hiding. Surely Dumont had no argument with children, but she hid anyway, trembling.

"*Peyatihk! Mon frère — peyatihk*," roared a heavy Cree accent.

"Stand aside!" Riel ordered. "We will search for the enemy. We'll take who we please!"

"Don't start another fight, not here," the Cree man rumbled like a waterfall.

"Marie!" Marguerite squeaked. "That's Sisebwepew. Mama's cousin. He showed us the Dakota horses."

Marie hushed the little girl.

"Marguerite is right." Jerome now, loud as a bluejay. "He talks just like thunder sounds."

"Ha!" Gabriel cried triumphantly. "Voices upstairs. Come with us, Sisebwepew. The rest of you block the back door."

"See! It is Mama's cousin." Too late, Marie claps her hand over Jerome's mouth. The stairwell fills with pounding feet; Marie shrivels back inside the cupboard.

"Here, bring the lantern. A bed, still warm." Riel tracking them. Light shoots through the cracks in the wood panelling. A rifle butt bangs on the counter top, forcing a reflex yelp from Marie. Then the cupboard door flings back and a massive brown head, long braids and a muscular shoulder thrust into her very face.

"*Bonjour Monsieur*," Marguerite said politely. "You have found us. It was Marie who made us hide, you know."

Marie stared in open-mouthed shock at the little snitch.

"Did she?" the huge man asked seriously. "Thank you for telling me, Marguerite. Would you like to come out?"

They stumbled from the cupboard into the lantern light. Louis Riel regarded them blankly but Gabriel Dumont's black eyes flashed. Marie tried unsuccessfully not to stare at his rifle.

"Monsieur Riel, Gabriel," Sisebwepew bowed solemnly. "*Permettez moi, vous presenter* Marguerite, Marie *et* Jerome? These are your hidden enemies who also happen to be my cousin's children."

"NOT Marie," Marguerite corrected. "She's not really our sister but we love her just like she *was* our sister. And she takes good care of us."

Marie felt tears suddenly threatening and looked down, blinking rapidly.

Gabriel Dumont's roar of laughter was even louder than his earlier bellow. His flashing eyes twinkled now and he laid his rifle down on the counter. He whisked Marguerite up into his arms.

"Mademoiselle Marguerite, I apologize for disturbing your sleep. It was very, very rude of me."

Marguerite's courage finally failed her. She buried her tiny face into his shoulder and said in a ladybug voice, "I forgive you, Gabriel."

9
THE LADY

Sometimes a short whoosh of air like a miniature cyclone would warn them. Other times
the shell would explode with no warning at all.
This time two shells landed with a thundering
crash so close that they punched the air out of
Luc's chest. A storm of dust swept over their pit
as a whining hunk of shrapnel thudded into the
log above his head.

"Holy Father preserve us!" Moise shouted.
Eleazar coughed and spat, then coughed again.

Luc brushed debris from his shotgun. "Nothing
we can do to stop them."

"*Peut être.*" Moise lit his pipe and sat in the
bottom of the pit. "Have a look with your young
eyes and tell me where the soldiers are."

Luc peered through the gap in the logs and
studied the enemy infantry lines.

"Black Devils are still over on the left, two hundred metres past the church. They have one cannon with them," he said.

"How close are they to their cannon?" Moise asked.

"Right beside it," Luc replied. "Then the redcoats are in front of us, about two hundred metres, maybe even closer to the cemetery," he continued. The enemy line fired some shots as he spoke and the Métis pits in front of the cemetery answered.

"And their guns?"

Luc squinted, trying to estimate the distance accurately. "They have two cannons about two hundred metres behind them."

The sound of running feet interrupted the conversation.

"Watch out!"

A man leaped through the air and landed squarely on top of Moise — it was Luc's father.

"Hey! Goyette, you've broken my pipe!" Moise pushed him away.

"Thank heaven you're alive." Adrien crouched, panting from his run. "We saw the cannon shells explode. It looked like they went straight into your trench."

"They were close enough to scare old Moise," Eleazar answered. "So we have decided to stop the cannons. Luc has spotted a weakness in the redcoat lines."

Luc looked back through the logs again. "I did?"

"The infantry have advanced two hundred metres in front of the cannon," Moise winked at Luc. "A perfect opportunity, eh?"

"For what?" Luc sank back down into the trench and pulled a lump of bannock from his food bag.

"For us to send a raiding party down the riverbank." Eleazar passed more tobacco to Moise. "We creep along the river shore beneath the enemy lines then climb up the bank opposite the guns."

"Of course!" Luc sat up straight. "We rush the guns from behind and destroy their firing breeches before the redcoats out front know what's happened."

"See? I told you," Moise sucked on the broken pipe stem. "The boy is a military genius. Unfortunately it's young men for the raiding party. Us old ones will shoot at the infantry — keep them busy."

Two more blasts shook the earth near the cemetery and a shattered poplar stump cartwheeled through the air.

"Excellent, Tom, you've made a first-rate job of it." Lieutenant Alderson crawled rapidly across the short grass, his sword dragging behind him. The movement caused a flurry of rebel gunshots from the trees on the other side of the church. One of the slugs smacked into the sod barricade Tom had erected.

"I'm spending more time digging that I am playing my bugle." Tom deflected the compliment. "Dig all night at the Zareba and dig all morning out here." He finished sawing a fresh square of earth with his bayonet. He tugged it free and slapped it up on top of the little wall that protected them.

"Well, our hole is now nearly a foot deep with a solid half foot barricade above." Alderson patted the dirt affectionately and lay flat behind it. "Pretty good construction I'd say, considering they've been shooting at the builder."

Tom smiled grimly. Here they were again, providing targets for hidden marksmen. There was no chance to hit back much less beat the rebels. Although Snell, for one, was using up a lot of ammunition trying.

"Lieutenant!" Snell called from the small shelter he had clawed out of the prairie. "If you'd just move around out in the open again to draw their fire, I could get a proper bead on their gun smoke."

"Brilliant idea! Capital suggestion, Corporal," Alderson laughed easily.

"Aye, you're a fine young gentleman, sir," Alex shouted from farther down their firing line. "But yon Corporal's a loon — take nae notice of him."

Ever since his close call at the coulee, Alderson seemed irresistibly happy. It was as though being shot at had given him a confidence he'd never known before. The men now accepted his orders with little complaint and joked with him. He had come to life on the battlefield — his stutter had almost disappeared.

Their good humour had the opposite effect on Tom. Another day wasted, another tent full of casualties and nothing to show for it. He peeked over the edge of their shallow scraping. Two hundred metres of open prairie; then the church and priest house; then the woods full of rebels protecting the trail to Batoche. They wouldn't kill a single enemy from here. Paddy would never rest — never.

Tom stabbed his bayonet savagely into the dirt. He wrenched it out and rammed it back down again. Alderson pretended not to notice but he couldn't help worrying. Would his bugler do something crazy? The boy's eyes glared from a filthy face and his knuckles were white where they gripped the long knife.

A narrow path curved like a tunnel through the thick bush just up from the river's edge. Far above them the top of the bank led to the open prairie where the Englishmen shot at the Métis trenches. Ten Métis men trotted single file like a wolf pack through the trees.

They paused; a dribble of sweat ran down Luc's back. The cannon roared again but now the din was behind them. Adrien smiled a wolfish grin and pointed up. They scrambled to the top of the bank and there it was, not fifty metres away, the

Canadian gun position. Adrien signalled and they dropped down again below the crest.

"Remember now. One volley, then we rush. Once we have the guns in our possession I will pack the barrels with a powder charge and plug them. You cover me. Then the fuse is lit and every man run like hell back to the river."

He shouldered his rifle and climbed to the prairie. Luc followed him. It was going so fast, should they slow down? Think about . . .

Adrien fired and the other shots followed in rapid succession. Luc pulled one trigger — saving his second, just in case. An artillery horse screamed and went down. A soldier, pushing the long wood ramrod down one gun barrel, reeled backwards and fell flat.

Adrien, screaming at full power, led his men at a dead run for the guns. Some of the gunners were still ducking from the volley; others stared in shock at the rebel charge. Luc shrieked his fear down as he sprinted after his father. Now the artillerymen began to scramble toward the limbers for their rifles but Luc sensed that they were too late already. He ran on with confidence — only twenty metres more and the Métis would have the guns!

Father and four others had reloaded. They fired wildly on the run. This second volley did no damage but the soldiers were forced to dive for cover — they couldn't make a stand now. Luc could feel their resolve breaking. The last of his fear slid away and a fierce surge of pride sped him forward to the cannons.

"A *droit! Regarde a Droit!*" a Métis voice bellowed.

Luc glanced over his right shoulder and an involuntary grunt escaped him — he felt as though he'd been punched in the stomach. The English Gatling gun. Its cluster of eight barrels and one of its wheels were plainly visible on the edge of a poplar bluff a little over a hundred metres from the cannons. Two soldiers were busy swinging it around to point at the rebel attack while a third man in civilian clothes fitted a long brass magazine full of bullets onto the top of the barrels.

Just the sight of the evil weapon took the wind out of the charge. Adrien extended his arm. "*Arrête! Arrête!*" he cried.

So close! They'd come so close to the artillery and now the machine gun would chase them off. It could spray a swarm of fifty bullets into the attackers in a matter of seconds. Already it was aimed at them and the civilian was reaching for the firing handle. They had no choice.

"*Sauve qui peut!*" Adrien roared. "To the river!"

The men turned and raced for safety. Luc raised his shotgun in frustration and fired his last round. The slug threw sparks from the heavy, black cannon barrel then ricocheted whining into the air.

"LUUUC!"

Father had nearly reached the riverbank. No protection on the bare prairie — no friends nearby — the Gatling trained on him — its handle beginning to crank. Blind fear returned, almost like an old friend. It put the strength of a racehorse into his legs and he ran for the river, scarcely conscious of his feet touching the ground.

"DOWN!" Father's scream. Luc smashes to the ground, rolling from his momentum.

BANG-BANG-BANG-BANG-BANG

The Gatling shots come in a connected string, snapping loudly through the air above him. A half dozen bullets kick into the earth simultaneously. Impossible to dodge or elude this devil.

Then silence. The civilian struggles with the brass magazine. A blockage.

Up and run, fly for your life. Eyes focussed on the edge of the prairie where the ground drops down into the wooded safety of the river. Run on with mother's prayer throbbing in your head like a drumbeat. Marie's voice chants the words:

"Lamb of God who takes away the sin of the world, have mercy on us . . . "

BANG-BANG-BANG-BANG

A clatter of bullets whip past. Too late to duck, too late to crouch, run and pray for the river.

"Lamb of God who takes away the sin of the world, have mercy on us."

Jump! Soar like a hawk over the edge. Fall for one long heart-stopping second before crashing into the bush below. Then safe. Wild cheering from his friends and a bear hug from Father. Safe when he should have been dead. Too much to comprehend.

"Gatling gun! Ha!" Adrien jokes. "More like *rababoo!*"

Laugh with the men and forget. Forget now and forever the feeling of those bullets searching for your back and missing by the width of a hair.

❧ ❧ ❧

Inside the rectory they would be protected. Just stay inside, Marie thought. A tearing rip of rifle fire burst from the Métis pits behind the rectory, and on its heels a cannon thump mixed with snapping bullets answered from the Canadian Army beyond the church. The church and rectory were centred between the front lines but both sides took care not to hit the Catholic buildings. Not deliberately anyway — three high-flying rounds had punctured the attic. Marie's cross still stood atop the church, unscathed.

"Marie, please." Sister Alphonsine pulled her back from the window. "Can you fetch me some water from the cistern? I think soup will be best today."

The nun gave Marie an enamel pitcher. Alphonsine was lucky — she had a proper job preparing the food. Sitting in a dank cellar with cranky children all morning had chewed up Marie's nerves. She'd come up to see the sun and check on her cross.

"I'll help you, Marie," Marguerite sang.

"Oh no!" Marie turned around. "I've told you and I've TOLD you to stay below."

"Father Moulin said the same thing to you."

Marie herded Marguerite back down the cellar. She lifted the tin lid off the cistern and reached into the tank — the jug hit bottom with a clunk. She tried again. *CLUNK*. Nobody had bothered to bring water last night after the soldiers retreated. Counting priests, nuns, children and sick, there were fifteen people in the rectory. There wasn't enough water for drinking, much less cooking. She flew upstairs, aware that once again the children had disobeyed and were following her.

"Sister Alphonsine! The cistern is empty!"

She might as well have thrown a lightning bolt into the kitchen. The entire household flocked to the room and a squabble immediately ignited. Loud accusations and denials gradually slid into quiet apologies and regrets. It was either everyone's fault or nobody's. There was no water and no way of telling when the battle would lift to allow them to reach the well. Those were the simple facts. Marie licked her lips, imagining that she was thirsty already.

"I'm the cook." Sister Alphonsine picked up two large buckets. "I need water to cook. I will go," she said flatly and marched out the door. It was such a simple, quick act of courage that Marie couldn't believe it had actually happened. The adults shuffled nervously and avoided eye contact. No one seemed willing to follow her leadership.

A moment later the door was flung open and Alphonsine rushed back in. One pail, a bullet hole gouged through it, hung awkwardly from her trembling fist. She raised it up very slowly, as though it was a trophy. Her eyes were wide with astonishment. Father Moulin went to her.

"Well now, Sister. It's going to be fine. No need for any of us to risk our lives. We'll just wait to get water tonight."

Marie took the buckets and set them behind the stove. Then she helped the shaken nun upstairs. "Here Sister, lie down on our bed for a bit. You'll feel better."

Alphonsine sat heavily and Marie unfolded a blanket for her.

"Merciful Mary Mother of God preserve us!" Alphonsine cried. "It's the Goyette children!"

She was staring out the gable window that overlooked the battlefield. A terrible knot tightened in Marie's stomach — she ran to the window. Two tiny creatures crouched like fawns halfway down the water well ravine. Marguerite and Jerome were caught squarely in the middle of the battle. They clung to each other in terror — their water jug lay in the grass beside them. A cannon fired from the far side of the ravine and its billow of dirty smoke rushed forward like a pointing finger. Marie recoiled in horror, expecting the children to be smashed by the shot.

"It's firing at the rebel pits, over their heads," Father Moulin said as he pounded up the stairs. "They're actually safe for the moment in the bottom of the coulee. How in God's name did they cross that open ground? How did they get out?"

Marie choked with guilt. Marguerite's plaits had come undone and hair was caught in the little girl's sobbing mouth.

"Quickly! Get me a white cloth, tie it to a stick. I'm going out for them," Moulin ordered.

"No! The fire is too heavy — you'll be killed!" Alphonsine shrilled. "Try a white flag from the window first to stop the shooting."

"Don't argue!" Moulin stamped his foot. "There is no time for a flag. I must go now."

Their dammed-up tensions burst, flooding the rectory with a babble of plans and arguments on how best to rescue the children. Marie felt bile rising in her throat and a wave of nausea flushed her belly. The floor canted crazily and she knew she was going to faint. She lurched into Father Moulin's room and leaned against his windowsill. The church swung into view with her shining cross at its peak.

Shining.

She concentrated on it. Bright sunlight reflected from the centre stick. Her sickness evaporated. A strange, light-headed sensation invaded her and she returned to the gable window.

There! Beside the children! A woman in a calico print dress stood with her hand on Jerome's head. Bullets flicked dust from the top of the ravine but she stood steady, smiling down at the little ones. The shooting slowed. Her face lifted and her eyes found Marie. They were gentle, compelling eyes.

Marie's fear shrivelled and a sense of calm crept in to take its place. She descended the stairs and opened the rectory door. Stepping outside, she set off without hesitation toward those eyes. They drew her surely across the grassy plateau to the edge of the coulee. Marguerite and Jerome had stopped crying but they didn't make a move.

Bees buzzed angrily past Marie and she wondered . . . not bees — bullets! She started down the slope.

The lady extended her hand. Marie hurried forward and squeezed it. Then she dropped to her knees and hugged the children with all her strength. "Thank you for coming to the children."

"You are very welcome, Marie," the woman replied.

"I should have been watching," she stammered, looking up at the lady. "It was my fault."

The lady smiled; there was no criticism in her expression. "Never mind — it doesn't matter now."

"You know my name," she said. "I'm sorry Madame, but I do not recognize you." She studied the woman, struggling to remember when they might have met. Her face was plain, with very smooth skin and her dark hair was drawn back to a tight round bun. The calico dress was clean but quite threadbare. The hem was ragged and patched.

The guns had stopped. A bugle tooted again and again. It seemed to hold the fighting at bay.

"Come now, let us take these two little lambs home where it is safe," she said, ignoring Marie's question. "The soldiers are impatient." She climbed up toward the church. Marie took the children's hands and hurried after her.

Tom stared at the woman strolling from the church toward the ravine. Violet! She wore a calico dress but no bonnet or hat. There must be a dozen bullets flying through that space yet she didn't even seem to know there was a battle being fought. He squeezed his eyes shut then looked again. It was his sister. Impossibly real. Not an apparition or a vision.

"VIOLET!" His scream pulled him to his feet.

She paused, turning toward him. He stumbled forward a dozen paces. She smiled curiously. He could see her face, even at two hundred yards, and suddenly she was *not* Violet.

"Kerslake! Come back!" Alderson shouted.

Tom returned to the trench. "Look there! A woman, but not my sister. By the gully."

Alderson's head popped up. "Your sister? Between the front lines?" he asked. "Where? I don't see her."

Tom knelt up and pointed. "Right there, just in front of the church. She's in plain view."

Alderson looked again. "EH? I don't — "

"For pity sake! LOOK!" Tom jabbed his finger at her. "In a calico print dress, not two hundred paces from us."

A storm of rebel bullets whipcracked around them. Tom and Alderson dropped as G Company let fly in return.

"NO! Hold your fire!" Tom shouted. "Civilian — Woman — Don't Shoot!"

"Well," the Lieutenant peeked around their protective wall, "she's gone now, whoever she was."

Tom inched his head over the embankment. "She's NOT gone. She's walking into the ravine. Order a ceasefire."

Alderson felt his heart sink. This hallucination was surely the end of young Kerslake. He was sliding into madness.

"Bugler Kerslake," he said gently. "Tom. Lie back and rest. Would you like some water? When the firing dies down I'll take you back to the Zareba."

Tom felt it then as surely as he felt the wind on his face. It was like that fraction of a second when an algebra problem suddenly makes sense — everything becomes clear. He knew he was the only one to see the Lady, and he knew she was real. He also realized that Paddy was watching her. The others were blind but that wasn't important. He saw, and Paddy saw, and she was Paddy's way home. The answer to Tom's questions stood before him in a calico print dress. If he could stop the fighting for a moment she could put Patrick Flaherty to rest.

Tom stood in full view, raised his bugle and blew "ceasefire". He breathed in through his nose without breaking the flow of notes.

Ceasefire — Ceasefire — Ceasefire — Ceasefire.

The horn chanted the order like a Gatling gun. Rebel bullets came a second later but they missed and he kept playing. Alderson launched himself in a flying tackle at Tom's knees. The boy staggered but stayed up. G Company's rifles fell silent and soon the rebels stopped shooting. Tom's bugle became the only sound on the field.

"There she is!" Snell shouted. Alderson turned and saw a girl with two little children walking rapidly toward the church, but she wore a brown dress and shawl, not calico. Snell's rifle rose and levelled itself.

"Ceasefire! Corporal!" Alderson yelled.

Snell looked back, surprise on his face. "I ain't going to shoot kids, sir. I'm just getting a bead on that damned rebel stronghold while I've got the chance."

The children entered the church and the bugle stopped. Tom dropped down to cover and Snell's rifle barked. A rebel answered.

"How did you know there were youngsters in the ravine — they were hidden?" Lieutenant Alderson murmured in a half-dazed voice. "Where did the woman go? Is she still out there? What exactly just happened here, bugler?"

"I didn't see the children in the gully either, nor the girl until just now." Tom shrugged. "But the lady went with them into the church, didn't you see her?"

Alderson shook his head.

"Well, Paddy and I both saw her."

"Paddy! What in the devil are you talking about?" The officer grabbed Tom's arm and shook him. "Are you saying Flaherty was here?"

Tom smiled. "Actually I just saw the lady, but somehow it seemed alright with Paddy too. You know?"

"No, of course I do not know," Alderson replied, mystified. "Are you certain you feel alright? Are you sick — headache maybe?"

"I'm fine, sir." Tom snuggled down into the trench. "Haven't felt this good in days."

The Lady entered the church, leaving the front doors open. Marie propelled the children in. They ran to the altar where the woman already knelt in prayer. First Marguerite then Jerome settled in beside her. Two little voices chirped "Hail Mary" in perfect unison. Their sound was unique — like robins singing in a choir. The bugle stopped its call and shooting started again. Marie shut the doors. The pleasant fragrance of incense filled the church; she took a deep breath. Her footsteps were loud in her ears as she approached the altar. The woman rose, motioning for Marie to take her place.

"I must go now, Marie. You won't forget me, will you?"

"But I don't even know who you are! What is your name?"

The Lady walked to the side door. "Goodbye. I beg in the name of my love for you, don't forget me."

Marie did not call after her. She found herself kneeling between the children. The wood step was warm where the woman had been. Warm as the sunlight on her face the day her cross had been raised. Jerome and Marguerite's voices filled her with a marvelous sense of wellbeing. She closed her eyes and drifted with their music.

Eventually Marguerite stood. "Can we go to Père Caribou's house now?"

Marie nodded. "Who was that lady, Jerome?"

"What lady?"

"The lady who came to help you at the well," Marie said.

Jerome skipped down the aisle. "We went to the well by ourselves — nobody took us. Then we got scared."

Marie caught his shoulders and held him still. "No, Jerome. The lady in the calico dress who came to you when you got scared."

"*You* came to us when we were scared," Marguerite piped up.

"The other woman — here, at the altar. Was that Madame Gareau? You know, her husband is the man who built the church, Madame Gareau?"

Marguerite shrugged. "I know Madame Gareau. But she went home to Bellevue a long time ago. She wasn't here today."

The front doors crashed open. Father Moulin, waving a white cotton cloth, burst through.

"*Petites diables!* Never do that again! Do you hear?" he bellowed.

Jerome shuffled his feet. "*Oui* Père Cari — Father Moulin."

"And you," he rounded on Marie. "Have you lost your mind walking into the middle of that battle?"

He stopped his tirade. "Were you hit Marie?" He inspected her closely. "You're pale; what is it? Are you faint?"

Marie shook her head. "I'm perfectly fine Father. You shouldn't have worried so much. The Calico Lady took care of us. We were safe with her."

"What is this . . . Calico Lady?"

"The woman by the well with these two. She wore a calico print dress. You must have seen her leave from the side door just a minute ago," Marie explained.

"I saw you and these little rascals come in here. Nobody else. And I can swear that a woman never left that side door." He held his hand up as though testifying. "You are mistaken, my girl."

Marie looked from the priest's quizzical face to the children who were watching her as though she was crazy.

"Yes Father," she said.

Luc's hand shook uncontrollably. He was thirsty again and drank greedily from the water bottle. He didn't eat because food wouldn't stay down. Battle images kept flashing through his mind — the shelling — charging the guns — racing the Gatling bullets. Echoes of gunfire still rang in his ears even though the soldiers had retreated two hours earlier. He pulled a filthy blanket from the corner of their trench and wrapped himself in it.

Moise and Eleazar were quietly singing an old hunting tune. He was glad the darkness hid his trembling fears from them. He drank again. He'd feel better in a minute if only he could relax. The soldiers were back in their fort, there was nothing to fear. Yet . . .

A sliver of light cut through the night. Somebody with a shaded lantern approached their trench.

"Luc? Moise?"

It was Mother's voice.

"*Maman, ici!*" he called eagerly, suddenly desperate to be with her.

"I've brought food and bullets," she said as she came up to the trench. "And someone else, too."

She moved her lantern so its narrow beam fell on Marie's face. "She wants to see you Luc. Go on, I'll feed these two old coyotes while you're gone."

Luc accompanied Marie forward into the poplar bluff. The trees had been so full of exploding shells and howling bullets all day that they seemed dead now and an eerie silence surrounded them.

"Remember what I said to you by the well? The night before the fighting started?"

"Yes." His voice broke. He breathed deeply to control it. "You said we must be brother and sister and that you might become a nun."

"That's right. Well something happened today, Luc." She backed away from him. "Something wonderful, in the church."

His heart sank. She had made her final decision and it sounded bad. "How could a wonderful thing come out of a day like this?"

"I can't really explain . . . ," she hesitated. "Père Caribou thinks I've gone mad, but I haven't. I don't understand how she came here, or even who she is."

"It has something to do with the church." His voice trailed off, afraid to face the rejection that was coming.

"Oh yes, Luc, in a way I could not have imagined." She suddenly seized his hands and squeezed hard. "All my doubts, all my fears are gone. I know that it's you I want. It has been all along, but for some reason I couldn't see it clearly."

"Me?" he croaked. "You chose me?"

10
VICTORY

J erome!" Marie scolded the little boy still
huddled under his blankets. "Hurry! Get up or
we'll leave you."

Jerome sat up. "It's still dark, Marie," he
whined.

"That's because your eyes are closed." Madame
Goyette prodded him. "Have you forgotten
where we are going today?"

Jerome suddenly came to life. "The caves! Let's
go!"

Marie helped gather their spare clothing into
the blankets which were then rolled and tied up
— one bundle for each of them. They had slept
on the floor of Xavier Letendre's shop last night
but now it was time to evacuate the village before
the big guns began firing.

False dawn showed through a large hole in the
east wall of Letendre's store. She looked from the

hole across the room. The upper half of one of Xavier's storage bins was smashed. A splintered groove had been carved across his counter. A second, larger hole in the north wall showed where the shell had left the store. What if they had been standing here when the thing crashed through? Maybe the next one would explode inside. She shuddered, and hurried the children out the front door.

Batoche's single street was already busy as other families made their way toward the river. One tall man bent under a huge backpack plodded up the street, away from the river. His wife and four children, all carrying large bundles, followed him. As they passed, the man pulled his hat down and deliberately avoided speaking to the Goyettes, but Marie recognized them — the Paquettes. He'd been fighting in the rifle pits near the church but now he was leaving.

"Another one gone," Hélène Goyette remarked. "I wonder how long we will survive?"

Marie didn't have an answer. A steady stream of Métis families had been leaving Batoche since the fighting began; they'd had enough. She remembered Luc's eyes — wide and staring. He had seemed confused when she explained her decision. She wondered if he could take much more.

Madame Goyette led them through the street and down the slope to the river's edge where the ferry lay beached on the mud. They turned right onto a path that led them a short distance up the shoreline to where the riverbank rose steeply up four or five metres. There were a row of black openings gouged into the bank.

"The caves! Look Marguerite!" Jerome squealed. "Come on, let's explore them."

He ran to the first dark hole and darted in only to reappear a moment later. "Aw, it's so small."

Hélène laughed. "Try the next one. That's the cave I helped dig."

Jerome shot into the entrance. "OOOh . . . it's huge! Marguerite — it's scary. . . . come on."

Marguerite set her bundle near the opening and crept in. She shouted, "BOO!"

Jerome flew back out. "Ghosts! Spirits!" he yelled in happy terror.

"Gather some wood please, Marie," Hélène said. "We'll build a fire out here to cook *galettes*, at least until the cannons start shooting."

Grateful to stay out of the dreary holes, Marie turned toward a poplar bluff. The east sky was now light with the new day. Whoever else might quit the battle today, she knew the Goyette's would stand and fight. Which meant that she would too.

※ ※ ※

"Only one cannon today," Moise said. "And no *rababoo*."

The single gun, stationed far away at the soldiers' camp, puffed a cloud of smoke and a half second later the thud sounded in Luc's ears. Then a quick tearing noise marked the shell's flight overhead as it sped toward the village. He scarcely noticed it. He was more concerned with the foot soldiers in front of them. They were bolder; their lines were crowding up on the cemetery and even those in front of the rectory were less than two hundred metres away. They fired at anything that moved; Luc, Moise and Eleazar stayed at the bottom of their pit. Luc knelt periodically to peek through the logs but there was no target worth a precious shot, yet.

He reached for his bag and checked again — only twelve cartridges left for the shotgun. Eleazar had sixteen rounds for his policeman rifle and he was hoarding them like a miser. Moise wore a cartridge belt over his shoulder. Luc counted the thin gleaming rims of the bullet cases that protruded above the belt. Eight. Moise kept his rifle, a Spencer repeater, fully loaded, so that meant seven shots in the gun with eight in his belt making fifteen.

"Forty-three rounds in total," Luc said. "Not much."

"If they were to charge," Eleazar said, stuffing tobacco into his pipe then holding a match to the bowl while he puffed it to life, "we could still push them back."

He sipped from their water bottle full of cold tea, stretched his legs out and leaned back against the side of the trench to resume smoking.

"But it would use up nearly all our ammunition."

"IF they came a second time . . . " Moise shook his head.

"They won't," Eleazar said firmly. "They're not crazy. Two charges over that open ground would cost them too much. They're happy to shoot their cannons and dig their shelters a little closer each day. We've got time yet."

Luc looked between the logs again. Beyond the narrow strip of trees a scattering of Canadian scarlet jackets showed against the dull grass. Many had built small earth walls for protection. Eleazar was right. Why risk a suicidal charge over the open ground when they could lay siege to Batoche — the soldiers had an abundance of ammunition. So there was still time for the Métis nation. But time for what? Eventually there would be no more food, no more ammunition.

"Listen, what's that?" Moise cocked his head toward the church.

Luc concentrated. A faint rumbling noise floated to him against the breeze. Then more clearly a rapid pop-pop-pop from the north. "Gatling gun," he pointed past the rectory. "Sounds like La Jolie Prairie."

"No, no, please not Jolie Prairie," Moise murmured.

"What's wrong?" Luc's nerves twanged. "We have pits along the ridge — I dug two myself. The Canadians won't get through there will they?"

For once Eleazar looked worried. "Pits yes — men, only a dozen or so. The English are at the back door and we aren't there to greet them."

A dozen! Luc stood in near panic. Those hills overlooked Batoche. Had Mother, Marie, and the children reached the caves safely? Or were they under Canadian rifles!

"Go Luc — run now, boy!" Eleazar pushed him. "The old ones will hold here."

Métis men were already streaming from the pits between the cemetery and the church. Luc ran after them. He raced down the ravine past the well. An image of Marie came to his mind's eye. That night by the well he had nearly lost her to the church — now he might lose her to the English. The thought spurred him and he sprinted through the tall grass just below the level of the plateau. He passed first one man, then a small group as he followed the edge of the ridge where it curved north toward the sound of battle. A volley of enemy rifles crashed loudly and was answered by a weak Métis return. Luc checked his cartridges as he ran, drawn to the gunfire again.

Marie patted the flat round dough and laid it in the iron skillet. It sizzled over the small fire at the mouth of the cave. She went back to fetch the next cake.

"That's all, Marie," Hélène said, shaking flour dust from the empty bag. "We'll take them out to the men in the pits tonight."

Marie counted the *galettes* — thirty.

"Even if we break them in half there won't be enough."

Madame Goyette simply shrugged. "Then some will go hungry."

"Not Luc, nor Adrien," Marie snapped, suddenly angry. "They risked their lives for those two bags of flour and they shared it with everyone — even Gignac and the Dumonts."

"There is still a little ox meat," Hélène answered calmly. "We can feed the children first then any left over can go to the men who didn't receive a *galette*. We'll be fine for today."

"Then we have nothing for tomorrow!" Marie protested. She didn't want to be a complainer but it all seemed so futile. Why struggle on?

"God will provide," Hélène said, nodding toward the cave entrance. "Perhaps *Uneeyen* has a plan."

A stocky man in a rumpled suit walked past. His face was covered by a bushy beard and his thick, wavy hair was blown into tangles by the wind.

"Gather children! Gather by the water with me to pray," he called.

It was Louis Riel.

"Prayer is needed," Madame Goyette snorted. "From a real priest, not him." She turned away.

Women and children began to cluster around Riel. Two old women carried a statue of the Virgin to a flat boulder that sat like a huge stone altar at the river's edge. They set the statue on one end of the rock and arranged a small thatch of crocus flowers around it's base. The statue seemed to draw Marie from the mouth of the cave.

"Can't hurt to listen to him," she explained half apologetically. "I'm curious to see how he plans to feed us."

She was curious, but not about food. If Riel was God's prophet as they claimed, then maybe he could explain the Calico Lady. She didn't dare say this to Hélène. Every time she told someone about the woman by the well they looked at her as though she was insane. But Riel was supposed to be different: maybe he would understand.

He climbed onto the rock and held his arms out in the shape of a cross. They fell silent and he looked down on them. Marie felt his eyes reach her with an almost physical presence; they were black and bright and unblinking.

"I have spent the morning in our beloved Batoche praying for guidance," he spoke clearly in a low voice. "The devil's explosions have crashed all round me seeking to frighten me away from God but I was safe in His protection."

A cannon shell landed far behind them at that moment and Marie flinched. It did sound like a noise from hell.

"Our table is nearly bare. There are those who grow weak in body and spirit. But we will be blessed if we do not let our faith falter." He raised his voice in a powerful command. "BE STRONG by the grace of God. Through Jesus, Mary and Joseph your confidence will be justified and we will emerge from the struggle loaded with the spoils of our enemies. Jesus Christ and the Virgin Mary will give us back our joy!"

His words came like a hot wind forcing Marie to step backward. Could this man make God defeat the soldiers? It seemed wrong, awfully wrong. His eyes lit upon her again and she looked down, suddenly terrified of them. Her hands trembled on her beads. The other women dropped to their knees and began to say their rosaries. Marie did the same, joining in their rapid prayer chant:

"Hail Mary full of grace the Lord is with thee," Marie whispered urgently. "Blessed art thou among women."

And it happened again.

Her fears washed away. A total sense of peace took their place. She heard the Calico Lady's voice inside her head. "Don't forget, I beg you in the name of my love for you."

Marie glanced up at Louis Riel. His eyes were closed as he recited the prayers and he did not frighten her. She knew he could not explain the Calico Lady but she didn't want him to. Not now.

"The General's angry, boys. In fact he's downright mad." Lieutenant Alderson allowed himself a smirk as he surveyed G Company's two ranks lined up near the north side of the zareba. "Seems the Midlanders and the Royals were supposed to attack during the diversion this morning but . . . "

"Midlanders probably got lost!" Corporal Snell earned a laugh from the whole company.

Alderson looked at Snell. "Let's hope not, because we have been ordered to reinforce them. We will advance under their command in this afternoon's operation."

He pulled a small piece of paper from his belt and read aloud:

"G Company, 90th Battalion will extend the right flank of the Midland companies. The Midlands and Royal Grenadiers will advance as far as possible against the rebel position."

Tom let the words sink in. "As far as possible". Did that mean an all-out attack or just more skirmishing? Had this morning's movements by the scouts and Gatling gun lured the rebels away from the church or would G Company be charging into an inferno?

The lieutenant folded the note and carefully tucked it behind his belt.

"So much for the formal orders," he said with a frown. "I have been instructed by Colonel Williams, commanding the Midlanders, that he and the Royals intend to storm the rebel line."

A jolt of excitement shot through G Company. Tom felt it tingle his backbone. At last, at long last their time had come!

"Sergeant Major," Alderson continued. "See to the ammunition and extra rations. Be ready to move in thirty minutes."

The company accelerated into a flurry of controlled chaos. Water bottles were filled; ammunition was passed out; hardtack was stuffed into haversacks. Corporals scurried about like sheepdogs herding their sections. Uncle Jim walked among his beloved soldiers encouraging them, checking their rifles and preparing them for battle. Alex and Walt bickered over the number of biscuits Walt had taken while Snell sharpened his bayonet on a whetstone and grinned like a hungry predator. Lieutenant Alderson argued with the quartermaster over the additional ammunition he was requesting for the men.

As bugler, Tom had no particular job to do and he found himself standing to one side as an observer. A surge of affection swept over him. The Winnipeg Rifles was no longer just an army title — it had become his family. These rough young men in green and black were his brothers.

They still carried Paddy on their roll call. Rifleman Flaherty would never leave the regiment now, never grow old, never retire. He would always be a young soldier.

The terrible dark urges that had plagued Tom were gone, and he could see these simple truths about Paddy. He thought of the woman in the calico dress. His hunger for revenge had vanished and all his pain was gone with it. Today, perhaps the boys from Winnipeg would confront the hidden rebels and crush their hidden fears.

On the left was the South Saskatchewan River: a greenish brown, broad strip of water flowing swiftly through steep banks. To its right two long lines of soldiers extended like a rope laid over the land. Nearest the river the soldiers wore red coats, then a small segment of dark green men, then scarlet. The red-green-red rope rolled slowly forward, rippling over small hills and bending around clumps of leafless poplar trees.

A graveyard, a church and a priests' rectory lay in front of the soldiers. The graveyard's crosses and broken picket fence overlooked the river. A path led from the cemetery, behind a long strip of woods, through a ravine to the church and rectory. The woods and ravine were honey-combed with man-made holes. Half of them were empty. Métis men crouching in the other pits loaded their rifles, watching the red-green-red line sweep toward them.

Tom Kerslake marched beside Lieutenant Alderson in front of the green segment that was G Company. They walked a steady pace, refusing either to hurry or slow down. Scabbards, cartridge pouches and tin cups swung from their belts, clinking like wind chimes. Boots thumped down the dry grass with a soft, purposeful rhythm. No commands were given — no orders shouted. The line advanced like a living thing.

They reached the patch of shallow trenches dug under fire yesterday and passed them without a glance. Tom stared at the long strip of poplars looming before him. Off to the left a corner of the graveyard fence appeared but no enemy shots broke the silence. The trees and graveyard were full of invisible rebels; Tom had dodged their bullets only twenty-four hours ago. They must be aiming down deadly barrels at G Company advancing upright and in full view, disdaining the shelter they had scraped into the prairie yesterday.

"Almost there," Alderson said. "The dance will start soon so I'll say Good Luck to you Bugler Kerslake. We will shake hands in Batoche before this day is done."

"Good luck to you too, sir," Tom said hoarsely, suddenly aware that his mouth and throat were dry as the grass. Should he reach for his water bottle or save it for later?

BANG

A smoke ball popped out from a rebel willow bush near the cemetery.

BANG

Another from near the church.

BANG BANG BANG from the cemetery again. Tom peeked to the left without breaking stride. The Midland line wavered and slowed.

Then a white fog swirled from the trees in front of G Company and a thunderstorm of gunshots sounded. The green line faltered in the hail and G Company groaned its dismay. Some men hesitated, others stopped to bring rifles to their shoulders and one flopped down clutching a leg streaming with blood.

"Steady boys — Steady!" came the Sergeant Major's voice. "Keep going."

Tom marched on with Alderson but the company was drifting apart into broken hunks of green. Many of the men had stopped and several were lying down in the false cover of the tall grass.

"Come on!" Lieutenant Alderson shouted. "Get into the trees. We ca . . . ca . . . ca . . . " His nervous stutter defeated him and he gasped for air. A half dozen more shots crackled from the woods, adding to G Company's confusion. Now Alex and Walt stopped to fire blindly at the rebel smoke. The Sergeant Major was shoving first one man then another, urging them forward, but it was like pushing water.

Tom's own pace slowed as he looked frantically behind him at the company's disintegration. The Midlanders and Royals were in no better shape. Fear seemed to reach up and tug at Tom's legs till he too stopped marching and knelt.

"D-D-D-DAMN IT!" Lieutenant Alderson broke his stutter furiously. "Listen to their volleys, they are weak. There's only a few rebels in there. This is our chance to finish the job, boys!" He grabbed Tom, pulling him to his feet. "Bugler, sound the ch-ch-ch . . . " He drew a huge breath and bellowed, "CHARGE!"

Then the bugle was at Tom's lips and it screamed the Winnipeg Rifles warcry. G Company shrugged off its fear and closed behind its leader. With a roar of defiance it charged bayonet first into the rebel woods.

Tom's bugle seems to keep blaring of its own accord. He crashes recklessly through the trees. Branches whip and ping against the brass bell but scarcely cause a note to waver. Rifle shots bark in front, behind and to his right. Dark green soldiers smash through the brush from all directions. A rebel rises from the ground. An old man with a grey beard and cold, calm eyes. The lever on his repeating rifle jerks and a billow of smoke spouts from the muzzle. A Winnipeg green body staggers sideways as the bullet slaps him.

Snell, screaming like a wildcat, leaps into the rebel pit. His rifle butt knocks the old man flat and his long wicked bayonet plunges down then rises back up, stained crimson. A second rebel, tattered shirttail streaming behind him, jumps from the pit and runs but Alex's bullet takes him full in the back — flings him face forward into the dead leaves.

Then the trees are gone. Open ground, the ravine and the church lie ahead. Alderson swings his sword overhead like a lasso, leading the pack. Red Midlanders, green Rifles, scarlet Royals, all mixed together, surge through the ravine and past the church. Tom's bugle is alive in his hands translating his fierce warrior elation into the call to charge.

A flurry of rebel gunfire from the far edge of the plateau has no effect on the young soldiers. The bugle pauses for breath on the high crest and Tom finally sees Batoche — a cluster of buildings in the valley a kilometre distant. Gunfire roars like ocean surf in trees at the foot of the plateau — the attack is momentarily checked. The bugle comes back to life: *go-go-go on* it sings. Charge again, down the long hill. Two redcoats, Grenadiers, stumble from the trees clutching blood soaked limbs. Another roll of gunfire, the screaming bugle peaks with it, then a cheer as the rebels give way and run streaming through the valley toward Batoche.

The soldiers stop, gasping, hurrahing and laughing like giddy children. Some shoot at the retreating enemy, most look about in the happy confusion of survivors and victors.

Then the officers begin their chant: "Don't stop — keep going — push them boys — on to Batoche."

Luc pointed his shotgun toward the cluster of English soldiers in the valley far below and yanked on both triggers. The stock bucked back hard against his shoulder as two barrels sprayed their shot out.

"Save it, Luc," Adrien ordered. "Your old gun can't reach them."

"Then let's go down where it can." Luc climbed to his feet. "We can't let them have Batoche!"

"It's over, Luc," his father said harshly. "Listen to me! We can't help them. If you go down there you'll sacrifice yourself for nothing."

Luc reloaded instinctively; his eyes were frozen to the terrible spectacle beneath him. He, his father and half the remaining Métis were indeed helpless — stuck on the Jolie Prairie hills overlooking Batoche, guarding the empty Prairie while the soldiers attacked below. He couldn't make himself accept it.

"Maybe we could sneak back into the pits at the church. Maybe Eleazar and Moise are still holding . . . "

"LUC, NO! See for yourself — they've been overrun. *misi wunichekitamowow*. Adrien rubbed one palm against the other. We must save our family — Batoche is gone."

Father's words hit like a cold splash of water. Luc's eyes cleared and his brain seemed to suddenly awaken as if from a deep sleep.

"Pack up, quickly," Adrien said as he rolled his blanket and tied it across his shoulder. "We'll follow the hills north beyond the village then cut west to reach the caves."

Luc tossed his few possession into his blanket and snatched it up. "The Canadians will get there ahead of us, surely?"

Adrien shook his head. "No, they will stop once they have cleared the village. They don't know about the caves and it will take time for them to reconnoiter the surrounding country."

Father passed his rifle to Luc. "Here, this will throw a bullet accurately for six hundred paces. Who knows — you might hit something."

For a second Adrien's exhausted face brightened with hope and a smile cracked the dirty stubble around his mouth. He seemed relieved. The Goyettes had done their duty; now they could go home and try to find some peace. Their war was over.

"One last shot for the Métis nation, my son. Remember it. Then we must hurry."

Luc fitted the fat cartridge into the Sharps buffalo rifle. He steadied the ponderous octagonal barrel, laying its sight on a crowd of red- and green-coated soldiers running toward Xavier Letendre's big white house in the valley below. They looked like tiny doll figures and he knew he couldn't stop them, or even hit them. His finger tightened, the gun jumped and Luc's last act of the rebellion closed. He *would* remember it.

A wild sensation of triumph carried Tom across the Métis pastures in the valley. The same ecstasy seemed to infect Alex and Snell, who jogged beside him bellowing wordless calls of victory. The rest of G Company, mixed with a tangle of Midlanders and Royals, flowed behind them in a rough skirmish line. Lieutenant Alderson's long legs kept him well ahead of everyone. No longer clumsy and stuttering, he loped effortlessly toward a grand, white, two-story house that lay on the outer edge of the village. Rebel bullets still snapped occasionally overhead but they were few and seemed harmless now.

Alderson leapt onto the porch in a single bound, bashed the door open with a kick and disappeared inside. A moment later a window opened on the top floor and he leaned out, waving. The young officer grinned as though it was his birthday party and he had just opened a long dreamed of gift. He flourished his shining sword and became the man that had hidden inside so long.

"Remember boys, who led you here today!" he called down to them.

Movement flickered at the far corner of the house and Tom turned, startled by the appearance of a man. He wore a battered bowler hat jammed down on his head, a threadbare vest and brightly checked trousers. He also held a rifle aimed up at Alderson, not three metres away.

Tom shouted a warning — a screaming cry for mercy. But his voice sounded uselessly a second after the rifle shot. The sword clattered down the porch roof and dropped to the dirt below. The bowler hat man sprinted for the safety of the river only to fall himself in a hail of army bullets.

Then Tom was in the upstairs bedroom with no recollection of climbing the stairs. Perhaps Paddy flew him up to Alderson; perhaps the tears in his eyes had simply blinded him.

Alderson's smart green uniform was scrunched around his body in a twisted mess. One boot was mysteriously missing, his foot twitched back and forth in its grey sock. The officer lay quietly on the wide pine floor planks and his eyes met Tom.

"Oh, Tommy, look what they have done to me," he said softly, rolling his eyes at his arm.

His right shoulder seemed to have been excavated to a bright red nothingness. His arm lay backwards beside him, scarcely attached.

"Well, I'm not crying," Tom said stupidly, wiping tears on his cuff. He pulled his handkerchief from his pocket and folded it into a thick pad. Then he took a breath, knelt, and pressed the hanky hard onto the pumping wound. Alderson whimpered and fell unconscious just as Uncle Jim burst into the room.

11
GONE HOME

Jerome and Marguerite huddled under their mother's arms like chicks beneath a hen. Madame Goyette rocked gently to and fro, humming a song to them. Marie pressed back against the earth wall and clasped her knees, drawing them up to her chin. Bright afternoon sunlight lit the entrance to their cave and seemed to make the dark interior all the more gloomy.

There had been a frenzy of shooting in the distance. Cannon shells began falling, some even exploding in the river near their cave making the water fountain upward before it returned in brief rainbows. Then nothing but a long silence. Another failure for the English attackers?

But now the fighting returned — nearby — perhaps Batoche itself. Men's shouting voices competed with the gunfire in a chaos of noise that lapped to the very edge of their shelter.

Marie imagined the soldiers storming her tiny village. Could the Métis hold? What had become of Luc and Adrien? The terrible suspense nearly pushed her outside to see what was happening. She gripped her knees and held fast.

There! A Métis soldier running along the river, searching for his family. Another and another! The sounds of battle slackened.

"Adrien Goyette! *Ici?*" Gilbert Breland appeared in their entrance. His face was haggard and wild.

"*Non,*" Hélène called back. "What's going on?"

"It's done, Madame," Breland said. He waved his Winchester toward Batoche. "They broke our line at the cemetery. We tried to hold them in the village. My God, we lost some good men trying . . . "

"What should we do?" Hélène demanded. "Should we go with you?"

"Stay here," Gilbert answered. "Wait for Adrien. I think he's still alive. If he doesn't come before nightfall then go downriver . . . " He rubbed his eyes and shook his head as if to clear his brain. "Oh Lord . . . I'm not sure what to do, Madame. I don't think the English will find these caves. Wait here for Adrien."

247

Then he ran from them.

The shooting had almost died out. An occasional Métis shot still popped from the other side of the river until two cannon shells slammed into the area. After that there was only the sound of cheering.

"Hurrah!" the heavy male voices echoed down the river. "Hurrah!"

Again and again the unmistakable bellow of victory came to the women and children huddled in their caves.

Eventually it subsided. Marie moved to the mouth of the cave and peeked out like a gopher afraid of a hawk. No soldiers anywhere, Métis or English. She resumed her seat near the children and fought the urge to run up to the village. She promised herself she would wait till the shadow from a poplar near the river reached the cave. If they had no news by then, she would go.

"*Ici! Louis, ici!*" a voice hissed from outside. Seconds later Louis Riel hurried past the entrance. Marie cocked her head at Hélène. She just shrugged, so Marie crept to the edge of the cave.

Louis Riel, clad only in trousers and shirt-
sleeves, sat in some long grass near the river.
Gabriel Dumont crouched beside him.

"Montana, Louis. Now! Before they guard the
trails. We must go south and no time to waste,"
Gabriel said urgently, taking Riel's arm. But Riel
pulled back, smiling.

"No, I cannot."

"Then we will gather up and fight again,"
Dumont slapped *Le Petit*.

"Gabriel," Riel murmured. Marie strained to
hear. "This is my time now. I am going to the
police. I will face the final act and I will face it
alone. You go to Montana."

Dumont began to protest but Riel stopped
him. "We will not argue *nistes*. Not now. It may
be the last time we shall see each other on
this earth."

They embraced. An impossible tear ran down
Gabriel Dumont's hard cheek. Marie sank back,
suddenly ashamed for eavesdropping. She turned
to Hélène and said simply, "Louis Riel's rebellion
is over."

Batoche's windows were gone. None of the buildings lining its one street had a single unbroken
pane of glass. Some walls had holes — tiny ones
from bullets and bigger, jagged ones from shrapnel
— but none of the buildings were destroyed. A
few soldiers wandered through the abandoned
shops even though there was nothing to see.
Anything that could be moved had already been
taken. The street was littered with debris: shards
of glass, pieces of wood, a wrecked cart, a smashed
rifle and a tattered blanket. A bright red set of
long underwear fluttered like a ridiculous flag
from the top of the cart. And on the porch of
Letendre's store six round biscuits were stacked
in a perfect untouched pyramid.

Marie took the top one hesitantly. She bit into
it. It was hard and dry but felt good on her empty
stomach. Most of the soldiers were digging
trenches east of the village and a procession of
wagons descended from Mission Ridge heading
toward the new army camp. She veered to the
right of the blacksmith shed and made for
Letendre's house. If Madame Riel was still there
she would know what was to become of them.

The setting sun struck her eyes so she didn't
recognize the object at first. A log perhaps, in the

tall grass near the path. She drew near and suddenly, horribly, knew that it was a man. He lay on his side, one arm grotesquely akimbo. His vest was stained red but his bright checked trousers were clean. An old bowler hat was still jammed on his head. His face was peaceful — that allowed Marie to tear her gaze free and run past him. Monsieur Ross, dead. How many others? Would she find Luc somewhere like this?

The thought nearly made her ill. She ran fast, gulping mouthfuls of air. Not Luc — please God, please Mary, please Joseph and all the Saints. She spoke each word as each foot hit the ground. Not Luc, please God, please Mary . . .

Marie staggered, finally out of breath, to the rectory door. Her feet had taken her past the Letendre house and deposited her at the mission. Sister Alphonsine stood in the entry; her cheeks were streaked with white, salty tracks of dried tears.

"Luc Goyette?" Marie blurted, desperate to know the truth. "Has he been here? Was he hurt in the pits?"

Alphonsine shook her head. "I haven't seen him. But Eleazar and Moise . . . they are gone."

Despair and hope fought inside Marie. The cheerful old men who shared Luc's pit — they had seemed indestructible. But Luc must have escaped or he would have been found with them.

"It's Father Moulin," Sister spoke softly. "He was shot in the leg. A bullet came through the rectory wall, barely missed me. It looked very bad."

Marie stared, stunned into silence as the nun pointed toward the soldiers' new camp. "The Canadian doctors took him to their hospital. They said they would try to save him."

Marie ran again, this time to the enemy camp.

The wounded soldiers were lined up waiting to see the surgeons. Over twenty of them lay or sat on the ground. Most were quietly smoking. They did not look at their bandages. Near the hospital tents five pairs of booted feet protruded from beneath five grey blankets. Shrouded dead men. A soldier walked past her and Marie plucked at his sleeve. He turned and she recognized him as

the one who had given Marguerite some peppermints at the rectory.

"*S'il vous plait, Monsieur,*" she said. "*Père
Moulin, ici?*"

"The Catholic priest?" He pointed to the
second tent. "He's in there."

She ducked through the low opening and the
sharp scent of disinfectant stung her nose. A
heavy stench of stale sweat and damp canvas
mingled with the medicine odour. A young man
lay directly to her right. His entire upper body
was swathed in bandages that held a large cotton
pad to his right shoulder where his arm should
have been. His face was a clear, milky white and
he breathed with shallow, quick breaths. She
looked away.

"Marie, thank God you're safe."

Père Caribou sat propped against the tent wall.
One leg was suspended high on a box and the
thigh was bandaged.

"Bad luck, eh?" He laughed.

Marie rushed to his side. "Sister said you might
not survive!"

"The bullet just hit flesh. The doctors are
going to let me go home tomorrow as long as the
wound doesn't become infected. I'll be fine."

Marie made the sign of the cross and sat beside him.

"Will you stay and keep an old priest company? It is lonely here among these strangers."

Luc and his father broke from the bushes near the riverbank and darted to the cave.

"Mama, Marie?" Luc whispered into the cavern.

"Luc! Thank heaven," his mother's voice replied. She and the two children rushed out of the darkness. She carried her possessions in a large kettle; the children each had a small bundle.

"Let's go now," she urged, pausing briefly to kiss him on the cheek. "I can't stay in there another second. We had almost given up on you."

Adrien took the pot and they hurried upstream.

"Wait!" Luc hissed. "Where is Marie?"

"She's gone to look for you, at the Rectory."

Luc ran after his mother. "Then we have to wait for her here, in case she returns."

"No," father said. "The soldiers are all over the village. They could come any minute — we've got to get downstream to Elie before night."

A confusion of thoughts raced through Luc's mind. Should he try to cut back through the enemy camp? Find her? No, that would be suicide. What if the soldiers recognized her as the one who helped him escape at Tourond's? They had already seen her on the first day and not known her. She would likely be safe. They wouldn't harm a civilian girl, but they'd shoot a rebel on sight. Or would they? *Think! Think straight!*

"We'll scout the church tomorrow, Luc. Maybe we can contact her through Father Moulin." Adrien pulled Luc after him. "But not now. Come on, before the soldiers find us."

Luc found himself swept along by their terror of the approaching enemy.

✂ ✂ ✂

There was just enough light left in the day to find the large poplar bluff in a hollow at the edge of Elie Dumont's farm. Elie's family, the

Chamberlands, Brelands and the Gignacs clustered together in a small clearing at the centre of the bluff. Straw had been spread on the ground and a frayed canvas tarp was tied to some trees as a windbreak. There was no fire, no food, and only a tin of cold tea that the children were sharing.

"Welcome to what remains of the great Métis Nation!" Gignac said, bowing and smiling.

Adrien shot him a look of disgust and turned to Elie.

"What news? Where is Riel? Gabriel?"

Elie shrugged. "Gabriel says to wait here. He will gather everyone he can and return later. Of Riel I've heard nothing."

"That's right! Excellent plan!" Gignac cried sarcastically. "Gather everyone here. Perhaps Louis Riel will declare another provisional government under God's divine will. THEN, this miserable straw bed will become the home of the *new* Métis Nation."

"Shut up! Whining *atim*!" Elie snapped, danger in his voice.

"Beg your pardon," Gignac sat down beside his wife. "Mustn't disobey the important Dumont clan." He whispered to Luc, "God I wish I'd never met the cursed Riel."

Luc spat very carefully, just to one side of Gignac. The very man who had called Marie a traitor and threatened the Goyette family in Riel's name just eight day ago, now disowned Riel.

The Goyettes burrowed into the straw. Luc, too exhausted to even stay angry at the slimy Gignac, fell asleep immediately.

⚒ ⚒ ⚒

"Luc!" Father shook him. "Get up, hurry. We have important news."

He instinctively reached for his shotgun, even before wiping the sleep from his eyes. The sun lit their clearing, now packed with Métis people. They all seemed to be chattering at once. Gabriel Dumont stood at the head of the crowd holding a piece of white paper. His eye caught Luc.

"Young Goyette. You read and write English." He spoke this almost as an accusation. "Read this for everyone to hear."

Luc laid his gun down and self-consciously moved to Gabriel's side. All eyes turned on him and the conversations died. He quickly scanned the message. It was a very simple letter printed in a clear hand. He translated it into French, calling the words loudly and clearly.

> *To Monsieur Louis Riel,*
> *Sir,*
> *I am ready to receive you and your council*
> *and protect you until your case has been*
> *decided on by the Dominion Government.*
> *Fred. Middleton*
> *Major General, Com'ding NW Field Force*

"Middleton invites us to surrender." Gabriel took the letter back and crushed it in his fist. "Some have already given up. I saw them with their white flags when I scouted Batoche this morning."

"What happened to them?" Gignac asked anxiously. "Were they protected? Is the letter true?"

Gabriel shrugged. "I have to say it is true. The soldiers took their weapons then set them free. No one was harmed."

"Then we must surrender too," Gignac said. "It is futile to go on."

"Go to the Devil!" Gabriel shouted back. "You can tell Middleton that I am in the woods, and that I have ninety cartridges to spend on his men!"

Michel Dumas and two other young men cheered, but Luc was empty of rebellion. He wanted only to find Marie and go home; there was no more fight left in him. Yet he couldn't bring himself to defy Gabriel openly.

"*Notinikew!* Come with me now," Dumont said. "The rest of you can go like sheep."

Dumas and the young men strode to Gabriel but the rest of the crowd stood in awkward silence. Finally Adrien spoke.

"Luc, your mother and I are going home. Will you come with us?"

Father's simple invitation snapped Luc's last tie to the rebellion. "Yes, Papa, of course." He went to his mother.

"Home, Goyette?" Gabriel said in a strangely quiet voice. "Your home will be like mine. Burned — smashed — destroyed. The English Army will have marched over top of it. You have nothing to go home to."

"We still have the land!" Luc heard his own voice snap back. His mother grabbed his arm tightly. "And we can work."

"Well said, Luc." Father actually laughed. "We'll start again, Gabriel, and rebuild. With our bare hands if we have to."

Dumont just nodded and turned away. The Goyettes gathered their few possessions and walked out of the woods going south.

The trail south from Batoche was as Gabriel had said. The Carons then Pilon, Delorme, and Boyer. Houses and barns in ruins, livestock run off or dead. They approached the hill that overlooked their farm. Luc ran ahead to see the worst. He crested the rise and looked down into the valley that sheltered his home.

A miracle.

The house, barn and shed all lay before him. They were untouched. A few chickens still strutted in the yard and some of their cattle were even in the pasture.

Then an even greater surprise. A thin swirl of smoke rose from the chimney. Somebody was using the stove! He began walking down the familiar path and the door burst open. Marie, his

Marie, ran to him. She took his hands, just like that night by the well.

"You're really here," he said. "And our farm — it's still alive. I can't believe it!"

She laughed. "The soldiers marched around your farm. They never saw it. It's a wonder, Luc. Really a wonder."

"But how did you know *our* place would be spared?" Luc asked, holding her hands tightly. "How did you know to come back here?"

"I didn't, Luc," she said, surprise in her voice. "That's what I mean. It's like a . . . a miracle."

He frowned and shrugged his shoulders.

"Father Moulin was hurt; I stayed with him at the army hospital last night. Then this morning I helped him return to the rectory." She pulled one hand free and touched the silver figure at her neck. "But something — I don't know what, a feeling I suppose — urged me to come here. The rectory is no longer my home."

"A miracle," Luc winked. "Marguerite told me that you saw a ghost at the water well by the church. Did a ghost bring you here?"

"Perhaps," she pushed him playfully. "Don't mock what you do not understand. It was a Lady that I saw, not a ghost. And she may be more powerful than the English Army and your rebel army combined."

"No more rebel army for me," he said. "The Métis Nation has fought its last battle."

Marie looked oddly sad at his pronouncement. He hugged her, swinging her off her feet.

"Don't worry. There's more to us than petitions and provisional governments. This is our *aski*, remember? Let Gignac go back to Red River. We'll not be blown away like thistledown; we'll survive, Marie."

12
WINNIPEG

A large crowd waited outside the Winnipeg
train station. It was a quiet, respectful gath-
ering of people who stood patiently in the thin
November sunshine. Nine shiny black hearses,
each with a team of shiny black horses waited
nearby. Inside the huge station the 90th Battalion
Winnipeg Rifles were formed into three ranks.
The soldiers wore smart new uniforms and their
equipment was clean and tidy. No battered old
coffee cups hanging from their belts or grubby
haversacks full of biscuit and tobacco. Their rifles
were presented in salute and the officers dipped
their swords.

A train huffed out the last of its steam beside
a wide, wooden platform. A minister wearing his
long white gown and cleric's collar stood on the
platform. Near him was a solitary bugler from the
90th Battalion. Tom Kerslake recalled that night

in the zareba when Reverend Gordon led them in prayer while rebel bullets whacked into the protective ring of wagons. He remembered how he couldn't get the hate and revenge out of his heart, even with a prayer. Then he thought of the strange incident of the lady in the calico dress. Almost Violet, but not quite.

A boxcar door slid open with a bang. A young officer, his empty right sleeve pinned to the breast of his tunic, stepped down from the car. Tom glanced at his bugle, shone into brassy brilliance. He touched the mouthpiece to ensure he was ready.

Left arm swinging, eyes rigidly to the front, the officer marched up to Tom and halted crisply. Tom saluted. Lieutenant Alderson's stiff face relaxed and he smiled.

"Good to see you, Tommy," he whispered. "I told you I'd bring them back."

Then he resumed a serious demeanour and gave his commands.

"B . . . B . . . Bugler, sound the lament!"

Tom raised the horn to his lips and blew. The bugle cried out its long, soft notes to welcome the last of the 90th's men back from the Saskatchewan territory. A single bass drum boomed a slow-paced rhythm.

"Escort . . . Sloooow March!" Alderson again.

One by one, the nine gleaming caskets were carried from the train. They moved in time with the drum. The first one was carried by Alex, Walt, Snell and Uncle Jim. Tom knew it contained Patrick Flaherty, and the bugle knew too, because it faltered and the smooth notes wavered. But only for a moment. Then they surged back, rich and full.

Paddy had come home.

FACT AND FICTION

The Goyettes and Marie are fiction. But what happened to them is mostly fact. It was a common practice for Métis to take people like Marie into their homes and treat them as family. Many Métis — like Adrien — refused to join the rebellion, and some sheltered with the priests in the rectory. The rectory was used by the Canadians on the first day for their wounded, and this made Gabriel Dumont furious. The real Father Moulin was wounded by a stray bullet when the rectory was caught between the front lines. They did run out of water and two little boys actually sneaked out to the well during the peak of the fighting. They returned safely but badly frightened.

Elie Dumont actually led a charge on the cannon, just as Adrien and Luc did, and it was the Gatling gun that drove them back. Women and children took shelter in caves, and Louis Riel held constant prayer meetings during the battle. Riel actually surrendered two days after the battle. Gabriel escaped to the United States and eventually retired near Batoche.

Although the Lady's appearance is fiction, two similar miracles occurred in the community in this time period. Thousands of people still make a pilgrimage to a shrine at nearby St. Laurent every summer. You will see the sign for the shrine on Highway 11 north of Saskatoon. Most of the Métis of 1885 had a very strong attachment to their religion. Their spiritual faith played an important part in their daily lives.

G Company is fiction, but the 90th Battalion and the Canadian Army fought almost exactly as described in this story. The *Northcote*'s voyage (complete with pool table), life in the zareba and the four (not three) days of deadly skirmishing all really happened. One teenaged soldier of the Winnipeg Rifles wrote in his diary that he felt as though he was on a "croquet lawn" in front of the Métis pits near the church. He used his bayonet to dig a small shelter then lay behind it all day under fire.

The army swerved away from the river to avoid ambushes, so some farms were saved. An artillery soldier — Gunner Phillips — was killed near the well ravine. His grave can be seen at Batoche. The final attack was started by the Midland and 10th Royal Grenadier Battalions. There is still some controversy over who actually led the unauthorized charge but it did happen as Tom experienced it.

A sad but true part of both Métis and English history occurred at the Letendre house near the end of the battle. An army officer named Captain French was the first man into the house and like Lieutenant Alderson he waved to his men from an upstairs window. He was killed by a Métis man, Alexander Ross, who was shot moments later.

The zareba trenches, cemetery, rectory, church and some foundations from the village shops are preserved by the Batoche National Historic Site. (I couldn't find the caves — they were probably washed out by 100 years of spring floods.) The names of the Métis killed at Batoche are inscribed on a monument in the cemetery. Many were old men who fought to the last bullet, like Moise and Eleazar.

The rebellion shattered the Batoche community. Some families went without crops for two years because of the damage from the fighting. Finally, it is very true that the young militiamen from the 90th Battalion who lost their lives at Fish Creek and Batoche were eventually taken home and re-buried in Winnipeg. Just like Paddy Flaherty.

GLOSSARY

Chapter 1

Notinikew – Warrior. (Cree)

Neya – Go! (Cree)

CSM – Company Sergeant Major. Highest appointment within the company for a soldier. (Not counting officers).

G Company – The 90th Battalion, Winnipeg Rifles was actually made up of six companies. They were identified by letters: A Company, B Company, etc. There were about forty soldiers in each company.

Chapter 2

The flour bags were called "hundred weights". They actually weighed about 112 pounds or just over 59 kilograms each.

Chapter 3

Vite, vite – Quick, quick. (French)

éclaireurs – Scouts. (French)

Mon Dieu – My God. (French)

Merci mon Dieu – Thank you my God.(French)

Ay-Ay-Mawinewhew – Challenge to fight, warcry. (Cree)

Chapter 4

Maskiki – Strong medicine/spiritual power. (Cree)

Hélas – Alas. (French)

Awas – Get out of my way!(angry). (Cree)

Notinikestamaw – Fight on someone's behalf. (Cree)

Nikawe – Mother. (Cree)

Kechiyimitowin – Honour. (Cree)

Chapter 5

Aski – Land. (Cree)

Kikinaw – Home, a place to live. (Cree)

Mes amis – My friends. (French)

On les mouchera – They will be destroyed. French words, Métis expression from 1885.

Chapter 6

Saketawah Kosiwin – In love. (Cree)

Hélène's song – This is a verse from "The Two Hearts", a love song popular among the old buffalo hunters. A young girl takes convent vows and her lover dies from a broken heart. The "Captain" in the song is not an army captain. The Métis called their leaders on the buffalo hunts, captain.

Sunka wankan – horse. (Dakota)

Kinyan – flies. (A horse that flies).(Dakota)

Une Soeur – A Sister, Nun. (French)

Deux vieux lapins – Two old rabbits. (French)

Snider Enfield – A single shot, .577 calibre rifle carried by militia soldiers. Obsolete by European standards but better than the weapons most Métis (like Luc) owned.

Little Black Devils – The Winnipeg Rifles uniform was a very dark green, almost black. The Métis and Dakota thought they looked like little devils when they attacked the Métis trenches. The nickname stuck and is part of the Royal

Winnipeg Rifles regimental badge to this day.

Galettes – Wheatcakes. (Métis/French)

Tareau – Like pemmican, made with beef. (Métis)

Chapter 7

Sakimes – Mosquito. (Cree)

Ekaya – Stop. (Cree)

Kipa – Hurry. (Cree)

Waniska – Get up. (Cree)

Chapter 8

CO – Commanding Officer. The officer in charge of the whole battalion.

NCO – Non Commissioned Officer. Corporals and Sergeants

Une Gosse – Brat. (French)

Peyatihk – Be careful. (Cree)

Mon frère – My brother. (French)

Chapter 9

Peut être – Maybe. (French)

Limbers – A two-wheeled cart towed with the cannon. It carried ammunition and equipment.

A droit! Regard a droit – Right! Look to the right. (French)

Arrête – Stop. (French)

Sauve qui peut – Save yourself (every man for himself). (French)

Rababoo – Literally a stew. Métis in 1885 used it as slang for something useless. They meant the Gatling gun made noise but did little.

Petites Diables – Little devils. (French)

Chapter 10

Uneeyen — Louis Riel. (Cree)

Misi wunichek tamowow – Everything is lost, destroyed. (Cree)

Chapter 11

Nistes – My older brother. (Cree)

atim – Dog. (Cree)

DAVID RICHARDS was born in Melfort, Saskatchewan and currently makes his home in Moose Jaw where he is an Instructor of Accountancy. He attended the Royal Roads Military College in Kingston, Ontario and graduated as a Certified General Accountant in Calgary.

David is winner of the Saskatchewan Writers Guild Long Nonfiction Award for 1988, the Sterling Newspaper Award in 1997, and *Soldier Boys*, his first novel, was shortlisted for the prestigious Geoffrey Bilson Historical Fiction Award in 1994.